R.L. STINE'S

GHOSTS OF
FEAR STREET ®

THE ATTACK OF THE
AQUA APES

R. L. STINE'S

GHOSTS OF

FEAR STREET ®

THE ATTACK OF THE

AQUA APES

—AND—

NIGHTMARE IN 3-D

TWICE TERRIFYING TALES

ALADDIN
NEW YORK LONDON TORONTO SYDNEY

This book is a work of fiction. Any references to historical events, real people, or real locales are used fictitiously. Other names, characters, places, and incidents are the product of the author's imagination, and any resemblance to actual events or locales or persons, living or dead, is entirely coincidental.

ALADDIN
An imprint of Simon & Schuster Children's Publishing Division
1230 Avenue of the Americas, New York, NY 10020
This Aladdin paperback edition October 2009
The Attack of the Aqua Apes copyright © 1995 by Parachute Press, Inc.
The Attack of the Aqua Apes written by A. G. Cascone
Nightmare in 3-D copyright © 1996 by Parachute Press, Inc.
Nightmare in 3-D written by Gloria Hatrick
All rights reserved, including the right of reproduction
in whole or in part in any form.
ALADDIN is a trademark of Simon & Schuster, Inc., and related logo is a
registered trademark of Simon & Schuster, Inc.
FEAR STREET is a registered trademark of Parachute Press, Inc.
For information about special discounts for bulk purchases, please contact
Simon & Schuster Special Sales at 1-866-506-1949
or business@simonandschuster.com.
The Simon & Schuster Speakers Bureau can bring authors to your live event.
For more information or to book an event contact the Simon & Schuster
Speakers Bureau at 1-866-248-3049 or visit our website at www.simonspeakers.com.
Designed by Karin Paprocki
Manufactured in the United States of America
2 4 6 8 10 9 7 5 3 1
Library of Congress Control Number 2009928750
ISBN 978-1-4169-9136-6
These titles were previously published individually by Pocket Books.

THE ATTACK OF THE AQUA APES

"You have the power to create life!" That was what the ad in the back of the comic book claimed.

"Pretty cool," Scott Adams said as he studied the ad carefully.

Scott sat on the porch steps in front of his house, reading comic books with his best friend, Glen Brody.

"Check this out!" Scott handed Glen the ad. It showed a picture of a mad scientist. He was peering into a giant tank of water full of strange-looking creatures. Creatures called "aqua apes."

"'Aqua apes?'" Glen laughed. He pulled off his glasses and polished them on his flannel shirt. "What are those? Swimming monkeys?"

"I don't know." Scott shrugged. "They look more like lizards to me."

"Well, what are you supposed to do with them?" Glen asked.

"You grow 'em. That's what's so cool. They come from magic crystals. See?" Scott pointed to the packet of magic crystals in the mad scientist's hand.

"Oh, right." Glen rolled his eyes. "Swimming monkeys from magic crystals. I don't think so."

"Yeah, well, they say it's guaranteed. Or you get your money back," Scott said. "They wouldn't say that if it didn't work."

"Maybe." Glen didn't sound convinced.

"You want to send away for them?" Scott asked.

"No way," Glen replied.

"Come on. What have we got to lose?"

"Three dollars and ninety-five cents," Glen answered. "Plus postage and handling."

Scott knew it would be hard to convince Glen to spend the money—but he had to. You see, almost all the kids in school could tell creepy stories—stories about totally weird things that happened to them. Like being chased by ghosts in the Fear Street Cemetery. Or getting attacked by half-human, half-animal creatures in the Fear Street Woods.

But Scott didn't have a single story to tell. Not one. Which, when you think of it, was the weirdest thing of all. Because everyone knew that if you lived near Fear Street, scary things happened to you. Period.

But Scott had lived near Fear Street his entire life. And he didn't have a single creepy story to tell.

Until—maybe now. If he could just convince Glen to send away for the magic crystals. . . .

"Such a small price to pay for 'the power to create life.'" Scott repeated the ad's promise in his best mad scientist voice. He wished he looked more like a mad scientist. It was hard to be really scary with blond hair, blue eyes, and freckles.

"Forget it," Glen declared. "First of all, I've never seen a swimming monkey. Not even in the zoo. And second of all, it's impossible to grow a living animal from a 'magic crystal.' In case nobody told you this yet, you need a mommy monkey and a daddy monkey to get a baby monkey."

"They're not monkeys!" Scott protested.

"They're . . ." Scott struggled to come up with an answer. "They're . . . something else."

"Yeah, apes. Aqua apes." Glen pointed to the words. "Same thing as swimming monkeys."

"Well, I'm getting them," Scott insisted, grabbing the comic book out of Glen's hands.

"So get 'em," Glen answered. He shoved his curly brown hair off his forehead.

"I will," Scott assured him. "As soon as you lend me some money."

"I'm not paying for some stupid water monkeys. You're the one who wants them."

"I'm not asking you to pay for them. Just the postage and the handling," Scott said. "And I wouldn't even ask you for that. But you did eat up half of my allowance yesterday at the Ice Cream Castle. Remember—your sundae to celebrate the last day of summer vacation?"

"Okay. Okay," Glen said. Then he stuck his fingers in his mouth and made gagging sounds. "I'll give it back to you."

"You're so gross!" Scott slid away from Glen as fast as he could. The last time Glen pulled this stunt he really did throw up. "Just forget it," Scott said miserably.

"Oh, all right," Glen groaned. "I'll pay for half."

Glen reached into his pocket and pulled out his money. He counted out three dollars and shoved it into Scott's hand. "Go ahead. Order the swimming monkeys. But when the magic crystals don't come to life, I'm not waiting for this stupid company to send my money back. You're gonna give it to me."

"Fine," Scott agreed. "But what if they *do* come to life?"

"Then I'll be a monkey's uncle." Glen cracked himself up. "Get it?"

"Ha, ha," Scott said, not at all amused by Glen's lame joke. "You'll see."

In a few weeks I'll finally have a cool story to tell at school, Scott thought. *And maybe even scary, too.*

Scott had no idea just how scary his story would be.

2

"No!" Scott shouted. "No!"

Scott couldn't believe his bad luck. It was the first day in three weeks that he hadn't been home to wait for the mailman. And sure enough, that was the day his package arrived.

But that wasn't the bad part. The bad part was that the mailman had just handed over Scott's package to Scott's older sister, Kelly.

Kelly thought she was the coolest thing on earth. She constantly reminded Scott she was almost thirteen. Almost a real teenager. Not a baby like Scott—even though Scott was only a year younger.

Scott and Glen chased Kelly around the kitchen table.

"We can do this the easy way, or we can do it the hard way," Scott said, closing in on Kelly.

He shoved his open hand out. "Now, give it to me." But he knew she wouldn't. Kelly never did anything the easy way.

"How do you even know this package is for you?" she teased.

Scott inched closer to her. "Because my name is on it," he said as he ripped the package from her grip.

"Jerk!" she huffed, punching him in the arm.

Scott ignored her. He couldn't wait to open the package. The minute the brown wrapping was off, Glen held out an open palm.

"What?" Scott said, staring down at it.

"You might as well just give me my three bucks back right now," Glen answered. "I told you it was gonna be a total rip-off."

Scott hated to admit it, but Glen was probably right. The box didn't look anything like the ad in the comic book.

There was no picture of a mad scientist.

No magic crystals in his hand.

Only lots of goofy-looking creatures. With

7

antennae popping up from their heads. And pink and blue bows tied to them. They swam around in a fishbowl, wearing silly grins.

"Maybe they sent the wrong box," Scott suggested, turning it around in his hands.

Kelly snatched it from him. "Ooooh, 'the power to create life,'" she read from the box.

"Give that back to me," Scott demanded.

But Kelly just laughed. "You two are such losers. What's the matter? Can't find any real friends to play with so you have to grow some?"

Then she tossed the box on the table and strolled out of the kitchen.

"So are we going to make these things, or what?" Glen asked, opening the box.

"I guess." Scott sat down at the kitchen table and watched Glen slide a small round tank from the box.

Another disappointment. The tank was nowhere near as big as the one the mad scientist held in the ad. It was too small for even a goldfish. And it was made of plastic.

The only cool thing about it was that it had a lid with a light you could turn on and off. And the bottom of the tank looked like the surface of the moon—with a big crater in the center of it.

Next, Glen pulled out some aqua ape food and the package of magic crystals. It was smaller than a packet of sugar.

This is going to be a total failure, Scott thought to himself. Then he asked, "How big are the ape things supposed to get anyway?"

Glen flipped through the instructions. "It says that happy, healthy adult aqua apes can grow up to half an inch long."

"A half an inch?" Scott moaned. "The ones in the ad were monsters."

"The instructions say we need distilled water," Glen said, continuing to read. "Got any?"

"No," Scott answered. "And I am not going to spend any more money to buy some either."

"Then you're not going to grow any aqua apes," Glen informed him. "Because it says right here that you have to use distilled water."

"I have a better idea," Scott said, suddenly feeling more enthusiastic. "Let's go down to the Fear Street Woods and scoop some water from the lake."

"Are you crazy?" Glen exclaimed. "Haven't you heard about the gross things that live in

Fear Lake? I know a guy who drank some of the lake water on a dare—he had to go in the hospital. Who knows what we'll get if we use that water?"

"Exactly!" Scott smiled his mad scientist smile. "Who knows what we'll get!"

3

The moment Scott came to the end of Park Drive, his heart started to beat a little faster. With just one step he would cross the imaginary safety line into dangerous territory—Fear Street.

Even in the middle of the day, Fear Street was dark and scary. Enormous old trees lined both sides of the street. And as the sunlight tried to sneak between some of the huge branches, it cast strange shadows on the ground below. Shadows that looked like they could swallow you up.

Once you've walked down Fear Street, Scott thought, *you know all the creepy stories you've heard about it are true.*

"The adventure is about to begin!" Scott announced to Glen. He took a deep breath and started toward the Fear Street Woods. They were creepier than Fear Street. Scarier, too.

The trees in the woods grew thick and gnarled—with black twisted branches that seemed to reach out. Reach out to strangle you.

Glen hesitated.

"Well, are you coming, or what?"

"This is a really stupid idea," Glen replied.

"It is not. You're just chicken," Scott taunted. Then he started flapping his arms and squawking at Glen. *"Bawk, bawk, bawk!"*

"I am not chicken," Glen insisted.

"Then come on."

"There." Glen stepped into the woods. "Are you happy now?"

"This way." Scott pointed to the path ahead. The path that led directly to Fear Lake. "We'd better hurry. These woods get real dark, real early."

As they followed the trail, Scott noticed how quiet the woods were. He couldn't hear any birds chirping or bugs humming. Or any sound of life at all. Creepy. Really creepy.

Scott kept his eyes glued to the trail. He had to

make sure they stayed on the right path. No way was he getting lost in the Fear Street Woods.

"Can we hurry it up?" Glen asked. He followed Scott so closely that he stepped on the back of one of his sneakers.

"Do you have to walk on top of me?" Scott complained, yanking his sneaker back up. "The lake's right through there," he added, pointing straight ahead. "Relax."

"I'm telling you, this is a big mistake," Glen muttered as they reached the muddy banks of the lake.

"Just give me the tank," Scott ordered.

Glen pulled the little plastic tank out of his backpack and shoved it into Scott's hands.

Scott pulled off the top and handed it to Glen. Then he stepped up to the edge of the lake and dipped the open tank into the icy cold water.

Other than being really, really cold, Scott didn't notice anything weird about the Fear Lake water. It wasn't gross, or smelly, or anything. In fact, it was clear. And Scott couldn't help feeling a little bit disappointed.

Scott held the tank out in front of him. "Okay, now pour in the magic crystals," he instructed Glen.

"I don't see why we can't do this part back at your house," Glen complained. "It's starting to get dark."

"Bawk, bawk, bawk," Scott replied.

Glen fumbled around in his backpack for the little packet of crystals. When he found it, he carefully tore the corner open.

"What do they look like?" Scott asked.

"Like sugar grains," Glen answered. He held the packet under Scott's nose for him to see.

"Pour 'em in," Scott ordered. He held the tank steady.

"Here goes nothing," Glen said. He shook the magic crystals into the tank.

The moment the first crystal hit the water from Fear Lake, Scott felt the tips of his fingers start to tingle.

Then the tiny tingling turned into a surge of electricity. It raced up his arms and snaked through his entire body.

He began to shake. Slightly at first. Then wildly.

He tried to loosen his grip on the tank. But his fingers were stuck.

The tank began to crackle with electricity. Scott could see tiny lightning bolts shooting through the water. The water bubbled and churned.

Scott's heart pounded so hard and so fast, he was terrified it would explode.

He opened his mouth to scream.

To scream for Glen to help him.

But no sound came out.

4

"**G**len!" The name finally burst free from Scott's throat. "Help me!"

But the moment Scott screamed, the shock stopped.

His arms and legs grew still.

The water in the tank settled quietly.

"What's wrong?" Glen asked. "What happened?"

"I'm not exactly sure," Scott tried to explain. "When you poured in the crystals, a horrible shock raced through my whole body. It was the worst thing I've ever felt."

"Let's put the top on the tank and get out of here!" Glen cried.

Glen shoved the top on. Then he turned and charged into the woods, back toward the street.

"Wait for me!" Scott screamed, dashing after him.

They didn't stop until they made it back to Scott's house and up the stairs to his room.

Scott carefully placed the tank in the center of his desk.

Then they both sat down on Scott's bed. Panting.

When they finally caught their breath, Scott bent down to peer into the water. "Oh, wow!" he shouted. "They're alive! It worked! We created aqua apes!"

Scott studied the aqua apes in the water. They were just little white specks. No bigger than dust specks in a beam of sunlight. But they *were* alive.

At first they appeared to be floating aimlessly. But when Scott squinted for a better view, he could see that they were actually wiggling. Wiggling in different directions.

The aqua apes didn't look anything like the picture in the ad—or even the picture on the box. But they were alive. And maybe they would grow into something cool.

"I don't see anything," Glen complained.

Glen was sitting on the middle of Scott's bed. "You have to get closer," Scott told him. "They're real small."

Glen didn't budge.

"You're not going to get a shock," Scott told him. "I carried the tank all the way back here and nothing happened."

Glen stood up and crossed over to the tank. "I still can't see them," he insisted. "Where's your magnifying glass?"

Scott pulled a magnifying glass out of the top drawer of his desk and handed it to Glen.

"Pretty cool, huh?" Scott asked, as Glen studied the little creatures.

"Yeah," Glen agreed. "They are pretty cool. But wh—"

Glen's voice trailed off as he watched little air bubbles suddenly start floating up from the bottom of the tank.

"What's going on?" Scott asked. He grabbed the magnifying glass from Glen and peered into the bottom of the tank. The bubbles were shooting up from a crystal. A large black crystal.

"What is that?" Glen asked. "I didn't see it when we poured the packet in."

"I don't know," Scott answered.

The black crystal continued to fizz.

Scott and Glen watched it for a long time, waiting. Waiting for something more to happen.

But nothing did.

The black crystal simply continued to fizz.

The black crystal was still fizzing when Scott went to bed that night. He left the light on in the tank so he could watch it as he dozed off.

But the aqua apes were way too small for him to see from his bed. He couldn't even make out the black crystal from that far away. But he could see the air bubbles rising from it. Scott began counting the bubbles as they rose to the surface.

The numbers raced through his head faster and faster. His vision blurred as he focused on the bubbles.

Then the light in the tank went out. Scott figured the bulb in the tank lid had blown. He'd check it out in the morning.

Scott pulled the covers up to his neck. As he rolled over to go to sleep, the light in the tank flashed on. And this time it glowed much brighter than before.

Scott turned toward it. *I should just get up and*

turn it off, he thought. But before he could even throw back the covers, the light blinked off by itself again.

Then on.

Then off.

It continued to blink on and off until Scott slid out of bed. The moment his feet hit the floor, the light in the tank flared on and stayed on.

He walked toward the desk slowly. Cautiously. As he stepped closer, he noticed that the black crystal at the bottom of the tank was bubbling furiously. The water began churning. It turned from clear to murky. Then dark.

Scott reached out to turn off the light in the tank. But before his finger touched the switch, he jerked his hand away. What if he got another shock?

The light clicked on and off again. Scott stood by the tank. Waiting. But this time it didn't flash on again.

Scott stood in total darkness. He wanted a light on in his room—now.

He stumbled over to the wall. As he felt his way toward the switch for the ceiling light, a short burst of light flooded the room—as bright and as quick as a streak of lightning. And then a loud bang exploded in the room—as loud as a clap of thunder.

Scott whirled around to face the tank. He could hear the water churning.

Another flash of lightning shot through the water.

Then the lid began to rumble. And before Scott could move, the lid blasted from the tank and shot up to the ceiling with a *crash!*

5

Where is it? Where is it? Scott ran his hands up and down the wall, feeling for the light switch. Glen was right, he thought. Using the water from Fear Lake was a big mistake.

Scott's fingers finally hit the light switch. He snapped it on.

He scanned the room. The lid of the tank lay on the floor. But from where he stood, everything else seemed normal. The water in the tank appeared calm and clear again. Nothing was out of place.

Scott stooped to pick up the lid. There had to be a logical explanation for what had happened.

Maybe something was wrong with the batteries, Scott thought. He pried open the lid of the tank to check. Sure enough, the batteries were oozing an oily liquid.

Scott crossed over to his desk to check on his aqua apes. The little creatures seemed to be alive and well. Only they were all huddled together at one end of the tank—as if they were trying to hide.

And the black crystal that had been bubbling and fizzing all day was gone.

Scott stared into the water. Searching for it.

He sat up for what seemed like hours, waiting for it to reappear. But it never did. And so, finally, Scott turned off his light and went to sleep.

"Scott! Wake up!" His mother nudged him hard.

Scott rolled over and pulled the blankets tighter around himself. He couldn't wake up. Not yet. He felt as if he'd just closed his eyes.

"Come on, Scott." His mother nudged him again. "You're going to be late for school if you don't get a move on."

"I'm up," he mumbled. "I'm up."

"Your eyes aren't even open," she scolded.

23

Scott rolled over and opened them for her. "Happy?" he grumbled.

"No," she answered. "I want to see you up."

Scott pulled himself to a sitting position.

That seemed to satisfy his mother.

"Good," she said as she headed for the door. "Now hurry up and get dressed so you can have a decent breakfast before you leave."

The moment Scott's mother left the room, Scott plopped back down and closed his eyes again.

"Mommy said move it, you little twerp," Kelly growled as she passed his open door. "Ma," Kelly screamed loudly over her shoulder. "The little twerp is still in bed."

"I am not!" Scott screamed back as he jumped out from under the covers. He stumbled over to check on the aqua apes.

They were still really small. But they didn't look like tiny little white dust specks anymore. They looked like *bigger* little white dust specks!

They're growing. Cool! Scott grabbed a sweat-shirt from his dresser. When he had it halfway over his head, he heard a faint tapping sound. *What is that?* he wondered. He yanked the sweatshirt down.

Probably just some tree branches blowing against the side of the house, he figured. He peeked out the window next to his desk. The tree outside was still.

But Scott kept hearing the sound. *Tap, tap, tap.*

He listened to it carefully—and realized it wasn't coming from outside.

It was coming from inside.

Right next to him.

Scott leaped away from his desk. Then he stared into the tank. And he couldn't believe what he saw.

An aqua ape was pressed against the side of the tank. And it was tapping on the plastic!

This aqua ape was big—bigger than all the little white dust speck aqua apes put together. Scott figured it was about the size of a tadpole.

Scott grabbed the magnifying glass and studied the creature. Up close, it looked even better than the picture in the ad. And it really did look like a monkey, too—all brown and kind of fuzzy. It even had arms and legs.

It stood there, at the bottom of the tank, staring back at Scott. Without a doubt this was the coolest thing that Scott had ever seen!

"Scott! Now!"

Scott could tell by the tone of his mother's voice that she meant business.

"I've got to go," Scott explained to his brand-new pet. "But I'll see you later. Okay, little guy?"

The minute the words came out of his mouth, the most amazing thing happened.

I'm imagining it, Scott thought. This just can't be.

Scott blinked hard. Then looked again.

No. He wasn't seeing things.

The brand-new aqua ape was waving at him.

"I'm telling you, he was waving at me," Scott insisted for the ten thousandth time as he and Glen parked their bikes in Scott's garage after school. "And he really does look like a monkey."

"Yeah, right." Glen laughed. "The whole tank exploded last night, and now we have a giant swimming monkey who waves."

"I didn't say he was a giant," Scott protested. He climbed off his bike and shoved the kickstand down.

"You did too," Glen shot back. "In the cafeteria you told Randy and Zack he was a *giant* aqua ape."

"Oh, right," Scott agreed as he headed toward

the door that opened into the house. "Well, he is a giant compared to all the other aqua apes in the tank."

The moment they reached Scott's room, Glen pushed past Scott to get to the tank first. "Whoa!" Glen gasped.

"I told you he was big," Scott said smugly.

"Big? He's like the size of King Kong!"

Scott laughed. He knew Glen was exaggerating, but he was happy that Glen finally believed him. "Is he waving at you?"

"Yeah," Glen answered as he picked up the tank. "He's waving like crazy."

"Let me see," Scott demanded.

"Wait a minute," Glen whispered. He put the tank to his ear. "Hey! You're not going to believe this."

"What?" Scott asked excitedly.

"I think he's singing to me, too!"

"You're such a jerk," Scott replied.

"No, you're the jerk," Glen shot back as he returned the tank to the desk. "There's no giant monkey in here."

Scott stared into the tank. It was true. The waving aqua ape was nowhere to be seen. *Where could he be?* Scott wondered. *I know he was there. I know what I saw.*

"I'm telling you, Glen. He was in there this morning."

"All right, all right," Glen muttered. "I believe you, okay?"

Scott could tell Glen wasn't really paying attention to him. He was studying one of the little aqua apes.

"Check this one out," Glen told Scott. "This little guy is pretty neat."

"Yeah," Scott said grudgingly, glancing over Glen's shoulder. "He's okay."

"Look! He's got teeny, tiny little flipper arms," Glen said.

"Yeah, kind of."

"Hey, cheer up. This is much better than I thought it would be," Glen declared. "At least it's not a *total* rip-off."

"But the little guy I saw this morning was *really* cool."

"This one is, too. Only he's more like some kind of fish thing than a monkey," Glen pointed out.

"Watch how he swims," Glen continued. "See him there?"

Scott nodded.

"He's almost at the top of the water. Now watch this. The minute he reaches the top, he's going to turn around and go all the way back to the bottom again, right next to the crater. And then, after he touches the bottom, he's going to turn around and swim all the way back to the top. It's like he's doing laps or something," Glen explained.

"Maybe he's training for the Aqua Apes Olympics," Scott joked. Scott watched the tiny little aqua ape turn around at the top of the tank, just the way Glen said he would. But he couldn't stop wondering what had happened to the giant aqua ape he had seen that morning.

Scott didn't have to wonder for long. Because just as the little guy reached the bottom of the tank, Scott saw a big brown hairy fist shoot out from inside the crater and grab it.

Then it tightened its grip around the little creature.

And crushed it.

6

"**D**id you see that?" Scott asked excitedly. "That was him!"

"Him?" Glen asked, staring at Scott like he was crazy or something. "You mean *it*, don't you?"

"No," Scott answered as he stood up straighter. "I mean *him!* I told you we had a giant swimming monkey who waves!"

"Yeah, well he wasn't swimming," Glen pointed out. "And I don't think he was trying to wave at us either. All I saw was a hairy arm that creamed the little guy."

"I'm telling you. It was him," Scott insisted.

"Maybe he just wanted to play with him or something."

"Play with him?" Glen gasped. "He crushed him!"

Scott studied the tank. But all he could see was some of the other tiny little aqua apes swimming around. "He must be hiding down in the crater," Scott decided.

"Maybe he's planning another attack," Glen shot back.

"Uh-oh," Scott said, a horrible thought coming to mind. "What if he's hungry? And what if he thinks that little guy was his food or something? I mean, he's so big compared to the rest of them—maybe he thinks they're *all* his food."

"Oh, gross!" Glen exclaimed.

"Well, let's see if he's hungry," Scott suggested.

Scott lifted the package of aqua ape food from his desk drawer and poured a little into the tank. It looked exactly like fish food, only the flakes were a whole lot smaller.

"He's not coming out," Glen observed. "Maybe you should dump a little more in."

Scott poured more than half the packet into the tank.

"Not that much!" Glen cried. He grabbed the packet away from Scott.

Scott stared into the tank. He couldn't even see the tiny little aqua apes anymore. There was too much food floating around.

Then something big and dark and hairy shot straight up from the center of the crater.

The water in the tank started swirling. Swirling like a whirlpool. And splashing out onto Scott's desk.

"Get the lid!" Scott shouted as they both jumped away from the desk. "And hurry! He's climbing out of the water!"

7

Scott and Glen stared in horror as a brown furry arm shot out of the bowl.

The water churned and splashed as the animal hauled itself to the rim of the tank. The creature had sharp nails, and they screeched against the glass.

Scott and Glen backed away.

Suddenly the churning stopped. And the aqua ape slid back into the water.

Scott approached the tank. Slowly. He peeked inside.

All the food was gone.

All the aqua apes were gone, too.

All . . . but one.

The hairy brown aqua ape floated lazily in the water. He was much bigger now—the size of a goldfish.

"This guy is like three times the size he was this morning," Scott told Glen.

"Yeah, well maybe that's because he just ate twenty pounds of food," Glen answered. "And everybody else in the tank along with it!"

"I really don't think he wanted to eat all those other little guys." Scott hoped that was the truth. "With all that food floating around the tank, how was he supposed to tell which ones were the flakes and which ones were the apes?"

"Yeah, well, I don't care if he didn't mean to do it," Glen declared. "He still ate everybody in there. And that makes him a disgusting little pig-monkey."

"A pig-monkey?" Scott laughed.

"Yeah." Glen started laughing, too. "We've got a swimming, waving, disgusting little pig-monkey for a pet. And all for three dollars and ninety-five cents!"

"Plus shipping and handling!" Scott reminded him. Then they both cracked up.

"So what are we going to call him?" Glen asked.

"Well, we can't call him pig-monkey," Scott said. "That sounds too dumb."

"How about Oinker," Glen suggested.

Scott rolled his eyes. "I don't think so."

"What about Hercules?" Glen asked.

"That's stupid," Scott told him.

"Well, what do you want to name him?" Glen asked, sounding a little annoyed.

Scott thought about it for a minute. He didn't really have a good name for a swimming, waving monkey who ate like a pig. But he did have a really good name for a dog. Only his creepy sister Kelly was allergic to dogs. So he was never going to be allowed to have one. I might as well give my dog name to this aqua ape, he thought.

"Mac," Scott told Glen. "We'll name him Mac."

Just then, Kelly passed by his bedroom door.

Yes! Kelly would have to take back every mean thing she had said to Scott about the aqua apes—and how stupid he was to order them.

"Hey Kel," Scott called out, trying to sound nice. "You want to see something really cool?"

Kelly popped her head in the doorway. "There

35

couldn't possibly be anything really cool in this room," she answered.

"Obnoxious as always," Scott mumbled under his breath.

"Oh yeah," Glen jumped in. "Have you ever seen a giant, swimming, waving pig-monkey before?"

"Yeah," Kelly shot back. "I'm looking at one right now."

"Whoa, Kel," Glen taunted. "You're almost as funny as you are ugly!"

Scott watched as Kelly strutted across the room. She sneered at Glen as she walked by. Then she leaned over the tank. Yeah, even Kelly would have to admit that Mac was about the coolest thing on earth.

"So what is it?" Kelly sounded bored. "An imaginary cool thing?"

"No," Scott said. "It's Mac, the giant swimming monkey!"

"Not in this tank," Kelly declared. "What jerks!" Then she turned away and headed for the door.

Scott quickly peered into the tank. Mac was nowhere in sight.

"I'm telling you, he really is in here. If you just wait a minute, I'm sure he'll come out!"

"I don't have time to sit here and wait for your imaginary friend." Kelly laughed her squeaky, mean, horrible laugh. "I've got *real* friends waiting for me."

Scott could hear Kelly laughing all the way down the stairs. He stared into the water again, searching for any sign of Mac. Glen moved around the desk, studying the tank from different angles.

Finally Scott spotted a tiny little air bubble rising from deep inside the crater. Then he saw another bubble rise. Only this one was a whole lot bigger, and it was rising a whole lot faster.

"Hey, Glen, look over here," Scott said, pointing.

Glen stared down at the crater, too. The water started bubbling so fast and so hard that it looked like it was boiling.

Scott reached out and touched the side of the tank with the tip of his finger to see if it was hot. It wasn't. In fact, it felt icy cold.

The crater at the bottom of the tank started pulsating and vibrating.

Scott's pulse began to race. What was happening now?

As Scott stared into the tank, the crater cracked right down the middle. Right in half.

And there was Mac. Standing between the broken halves.

"Wow!" Glen exclaimed. "It's Mac! And look at the size of him!"

"He's the size of a mouse now!" Scott exclaimed.

"Do you think he is going to grow any bigger?" Glen asked.

"How should I know?" Scott answered. "But this tank is too small for him now. We've got to find a bigger place for him."

"How about that aquarium you used to keep turtles in? Do you still have it?"

Scott hurried over to the closet and checked the shelves. Yep. There it was! He brought it over to the desk.

Then Scott stretched out on the floor and felt around under the bed. He pulled out a bag of blue gravel, a little plastic treasure chest, a plastic skeleton, and a plastic palm tree.

Glen grabbed the gravel and poured it into the aquarium. Then he carefully arranged the toys, planting them firmly in the gravel.

"Don't be afraid," Scott told Mac. He slowly poured the water from the tank into the aquarium.

Mac plopped into his new home and instantly began swimming around.

"Hey, great!" Glen cheered. "I think he likes it!"

"Let's go fill up one of the big pitchers my mom has in the kitchen," Scott said. "Mac needs more water."

They headed out of the room. "We'll be right back, Mac," Scott called.

Scott led the way into the kitchen and found a pitcher.

"You know what Mac looks like?" Scott asked as he filled the pitcher with water. "He looks like one of those monkeys in *The Wizard of Oz*. He's even got little wings on his back."

"Yeah, water wings," Glen joked.

They hurried back to Scott's room. On the way in, Scott stopped so suddenly that Glen slammed right into him.

"Hey, watch where you're going," Glen complained.

But Scott didn't reply.

He simply pointed.

And gasped.

8

Scott and Glen stared in horror at the floor.

It was littered with blue gravel. The gravel that Glen had carefully poured into the aquarium.

And the little plastic treasure chest he had positioned so securely in the gravel sat upside down on Scott's desk.

Scott searched the room for the palm tree. There it was—in two pieces. Half on the dresser and half on the bed.

The bones of the pirate skeleton were scattered everywhere.

It looked as if someone had picked up the

aquarium and hurled its contents out. Except . . .

The carpet wasn't soaked.

And the aquarium still sat on Scott's desk.

And it still had the same amount of water in it.

And Mac—now the size of a gerbil!—was still happily swimming around inside it.

"Did you do this?" Scott asked Glen.

"Are you crazy?" Glen shouted. "How could I have done it? I was with you the whole time."

"Well, it didn't just happen by itself."

"Gee, Scott," Glen mocked. "Really?"

Scott moved toward his desk. The gravel crunched under his feet.

He stooped down and peered closely into the aquarium.

"Hey! What's going on!" he cried.

On the bottom of the aquarium sat one of Scott's most prized possessions—a real silver dollar, dated 1879. And right next to it was his watch—the watch his parents had given him for his last birthday. Good thing it was waterproof.

Some pennies, a pencil sharpener, a pack of gum, and a glow-in-the-dark rubber ball were in there, too.

"I don't believe this!" Scott said, over and over again. "I just don't believe this!"

As Scott and Glen stared in amazement, Mac swam under the rubber ball. He pitched it right out of the water. The ball flew from the bowl, bounced once on the desk, then fell to the floor.

"Wow!" Glen exclaimed. "Mac must be really strong. Throwing that ball would be like us throwing an elephant!"

"Do you think *he* did all *this?*" Scott asked, motioning to the toys scattered around his room.

"No way!" Glen replied. "No way!"

"But you just said he was strong," Scott reminded him.

"Well, maybe he did throw this stuff out," Glen answered. "But he couldn't get the other stuff in there. There's got to be another explanation."

"Yeah? Like what?" Scott asked.

"Kelly?" Glen suggested.

"Nope. Kelly went out. We're alone here."

Glen couldn't come up with one explanation, Scott realized. And neither could he.

They both stared down at the aquarium.

"You know wh-what this means, don't you?" Scott stammered.

"No. What?"

"It means Mac can get out!"

9

Scott grabbed the aqua ape instruction booklet off his desk and flipped through it. *Are aqua apes supposed to leave their tanks?* he wondered. He didn't think so.

"Does it have a section on what happens when idiots don't use distilled water?" Glen demanded.

"What's that supposed to mean?"

"It means that we have no clue what Mac's going to turn into. All because *you* had to use water from Fear Lake."

"Yeah, well Mac's way cooler than those little white specks!" Scott insisted. "And that's all we would have had if we had followed the instructions the way *you* wanted to."

Scott stared down at Mac, his eyes growing wider at what he saw.

The aqua ape was busy stacking all the pennies on top of the little pencil sharpener. "I can't believe what he's doing!" he cried. "But we've got to get my stuff out of this bowl."

"You get it out," Glen said. "It's your stuff!"

Scott didn't want to stick his fingers in the water. He didn't know what Mac would do. But he wanted his watch and his silver dollar out of there. So he had no choice.

He decided to go for the watch first. Mac wasn't too near it.

Scott took a deep breath and shot his hand down. He grabbed the watch and jerked his hand back.

Scott grinned and shook the watch in front of Glen. Drops of water splashed across Glen's face. "Your turn," he said. "Unless you're too scared!"

Glen wiped the water off his face with his sleeve. "I'm not the one who wants the stuff, so why should I get it?" he asked.

Scott reached for the silver dollar, feeling a lot less nervous.

He dipped his hand into the water—and snap!

A sharp, fierce pain shot through his fingers as Mac clamped down on them. Hard.

Stabbing them.

Stabbing them with his razor-sharp teeth.

10

"**H**elp! He's got me!" Scott screamed.

Mac clawed his way up Scott's hand. It felt like hot needles jabbing into his skin. Tiny drops of blood spurted out of his skin.

Scott shook his hand back and forth. Furiously. Trying to fling Mac off. But Mac just dug his teeth in deeper.

He slithered under the sleeve of Scott's sweatshirt. Scott could feel Mac moving. Moving up. Leaving a burning trail on his bare arm.

"Help! Get him out! Get him out!" Scott jumped up and down, whacking at Mac through his shirt. "I feel like I'm on fire!"

"What's wrong with you?" Glen shouted back.

"Mac!" Scott screamed. "He ran up my sleeve!"

"He ran up your sleeve?" Glen repeated in total disbelief. "Gross!"

"Get him out!" Scott yelled.

"Take your sweatshirt off," Glen snapped back.

Scott yanked his sweatshirt up over his head.

He glanced down at his arm.

No Mac.

He figured that Mac had to be somewhere in his sweatshirt. But he was wrong.

"Don't move," Glen instructed him. He stared at a spot on Scott's chest.

Scott looked down and saw Mac clinging to the front of his T-shirt. Mac stared straight up at him. "Get him off me!"

Glen moved closer. But only to get a better look. "Cool," Glen said, inspecting Mac from safely behind Scott's shoulder. "Oh, wow. He's smiling at me!

"This is totally amazing," Glen went on. "He sure has sharp teeth. They could do some real damage. I'm not touching him."

Scott couldn't stand having Mac stuck to him

47

for one more second. It was like having a big creepy insect—like a tarantula—on him.

Scott inched his hand toward the aqua ape. Mac watched carefully, but remained still.

When Scott's fingertip finally touched Mac, he was surprised by what he felt. Mac's fur was just like any other animal's fur. Even though it was wet and matted from the water, it was still soft. And Scott could tell that if it were dry it would be fluffy, too.

Suddenly, Scott wasn't so grossed out anymore. He ran his finger gently down Mac's back, petting him. And Mac really seemed to like it. He leaned into Scott's finger and rubbed against it, making little squeaking noises.

"Let me pet him," Glen butted in.

"Oh, sure. Now you want to touch him."

Scott watched as Glen petted Mac.

"He's really neat," Glen had to admit. "I never thought we'd get anything like this when we ordered the aqua apes kit."

"You didn't think we'd get anything at all," Scott reminded him.

"Are you sure he's okay out of the water like this?" Glen changed the subject.

Scott shrugged. "He seems okay. Besides, it's

48

not like we took him out. He came out all by himself." With Mac still attached to his shirt, Scott gently lowered himself to the floor. He continued to stroke Mac's fur.

Glen sat opposite him. Mac jumped off Scott's shirt and stood on the floor between the two boys.

What is he going to do? Scott wondered. But all Mac did was glance back and forth at the two of them, as if he expected them to do something first.

"Maybe he wants to play," Glen suggested.

"How do you play with an aqua—?" But before Scott finished, he had an idea.

Scott spotted the glow-in-the-dark ball that Mac had tossed out of the tank earlier. He picked it up from the floor and rolled it gently toward Mac.

The ball came to a stop right in front of Mac. Mac stared at it for a second. Then he peered at Scott. Then he did just what Scott hoped he would—Mac picked up the ball and tossed it back.

Scott wasn't quick enough to catch it. The ball hit him in the chest with a thump and fell to the floor.

"I can't believe how strong he is."

"Yeah," Scott answered, rubbing his chest. "That hurt!"

"It was an accident," Glen defended Mac.

"I know," Scott said, "but it still hurt."

Glen reached for the ball and rolled it back to Mac. Mac picked it up and tossed it back to Glen.

"This is great!" Scott exclaimed.

Mac seemed to love playing ball. Sometimes he threw it right to Scott or Glen. And sometimes he threw it past them so that they would have to go fetch it. But when Scott or Glen tried to make Mac fetch, Mac refused. He simply sat down and waited for one of them to get it.

"Hey, do you think Mac is shrinking?" Scott asked as he fetched the ball for the little ape.

"Gee. I think he is. He looks smaller—and sort of flatter."

Scott rolled the ball gently to Mac. But Mac ignored it. He slowly crawled back to Scott's desk. Then, just like a bug, he climbed right up the side and pulled himself into his aquarium.

Scott stood and stared at Mac, who was now floating in the water. "Look!" he called to Glen. "He's starting to puff up again. I guess he can't be out of the water for too long. It wears him out."

"We should let him rest," Glen suggested, picking up his jacket. "Why don't we go to the mall and play Thunder Racer at the video arcade?"

Scott grabbed his jacket off the bed. "Why would you want to do that? You stink at Thunder Racer. It can't be much fun for you."

"You're the one who stinks," Glen shot back, heading for the door.

"You crash and burn every time you step on the gas pedal," Scott insisted. He glanced around the room for his baseball cap. He found it hanging on the back of his desk chair near Mac's tank. He grabbed it and stuck it on.

"Yeah, well, the only reason you don't crash is because you drive five miles an hour," Glen told him as they leaped down the stairs.

"First one to the bus stop gets the first turn!" Glen yelled. He shoved through the front door ahead of Scott and took off down the street.

"The only way you can beat me is by cheating," Scott called, racing after him. Then he stopped. "Hey, wait. Mac's aquarium doesn't have a lid! We have to go back and cover it with something."

Glen turned around and trotted backward toward the bus stop. "Don't worry," he shouted. "Mac's resting. Besides, what could happen?"

"**W**atch out!" Glen yelled. "You're gonna get creamed!"

But it was too late. Scott had already lost control of the video race car. He closed his eyes just as he was about to hit the wall. The sound of the crash echoed all around him.

Thunder Racer was the coolest game in the arcade. The seats of the car bounced around as if the car were actually speeding around a racetrack. The video screen in front of the car was gigantic. And huge speakers made everything sound totally real.

"Give me another quarter," Scott said to Glen.

He was having so much fun that he had almost forgotten all about Mac.

Almost.

He couldn't help wondering if he should have used distilled water to grow the aqua apes. He was afraid using the Fear Lake water had made Mac turn out . . . wrong.

"No way," Glen answered. "It's my turn."

"Come on," Scott pleaded, refusing to budge from the driver's seat. "I let you go twice."

"Yeah, but this is my last quarter," Glen said. "And it's my turn!"

"If you got to go twice in a row, I get to go twice in a row," Scott insisted.

Scott dug through the pockets of his jeans, searching for change. No luck. He tried his jacket pockets next.

But instead of quarters, Scott found something else. Something he hadn't put there.

And whatever it was, it definitely did not belong in his jacket. It felt damp and yucky, like a wad of wet tissues.

And then it moved!

"Aaaagh!" Scott screamed, yanking his hand out of his pocket.

"What's wrong?" Glen asked, startled.

But he didn't have to wait for an answer.

Mac leaped out of Scott's pocket and landed on the steering wheel!

Scott's jaw gaped open. "Hey! How did you get in there?"

He was quite a bit smaller—but they had been at the arcade for an hour now. Scott figured Mac shrunk because he'd been out of the water all that time.

Scott reached down to pick Mac up. But Mac was too fast. He jumped onto the side of the car and dived into the coin return slot.

"Uh-oh," Glen gasped. "How are we gonna get him out of there?"

"I don't know," Scott groaned, peering down into the slot.

"Maybe this will work," Glen said. He pushed the coin return button.

Mac didn't come back out. But a quarter did.

"Cool," Glen said, reaching for the quarter. But before he could pick it up, another quarter dropped out.

And then another.

And another.

Then quarters started pouring out of the machine.

"Oh, no," Scott moaned, trying to shove the quarters back in. "It looks like Mac broke the machine."

Glen pushed Scott's hands out of the way so the quarters could keep coming. "So what's the problem? This is great!" Glen exclaimed as he scooped up a handful of change.

"Hey! You!" a really deep, really mean voice called from behind them. "What do you two clowns think you're doing over there?"

Scott and Glen turned toward the voice.

"Uh-oh. It's the manager—Big Bruno," Scott whispered. "And he's heading this way!"

12

"**W**e've got to get out of here!" Scott cried.

The manager stomped through the crowds of kids. Getting closer and closer.

"What about Mac?" Glen asked. "We can't just leave him here!"

As if he heard Glen, the aqua ape popped out of the coin slot as quickly as he'd jumped in.

"Here he is," Scott cried, spotting Mac. He reached out for him but Mac was too fast. He sprang from the top of the coin slot to the floor. Then he scurried away.

Scott and Glen charged after Mac. Scott glanced over his shoulder—and breathed a long sigh of relief. The manager wasn't chasing them. He was too busy picking up all the quarters they'd left behind.

That was the good news. The bad news was that Mac was lost in a sea of sneakers. Sneakers attached to kids who were playing video games— yelling, screaming, and jumping. Jumping up and down in excitement. Pounding the floor. Narrowly missing Mac as he weaved in between them.

Nobody seemed to notice Mac as he zigzagged through the crowd.

"Look out!" Scott yelled as a tall, stocky kid with major muscles almost smashed Mac flat.

Mac dove over the shoe and escaped. But Scott ran right into the kid. "Look out, yourself," the kid snarled, shoving Scott hard.

Scott fell backward into Glen. Then they both tumbled to the floor. By the time they scrambled to their feet, they had lost sight of Mac.

"Oh, no!" Scott cried. "Where is he?"

"I don't see him anywhere," Glen answered.

Then, suddenly, a pinball machine near Scott came alive—all by itself.

The balls started zinging around inside.

The lights flashed on and off.

Bells clanged.

Buzzers buzzed.

Scott had the terrible feeling that he knew exactly where Mac was.

And he could tell Glen was thinking the same thing. Glen leaned over and peeked into the coin return slot.

"Can you see anything?" Scott asked. The balls began zipping around the machine faster and faster. Bouncing off the bumpers. Disappearing down secret traps, then popping out again. The bells clanged louder as more balls flew—flew around the machine, which was shaking madly now. It looked as if it were about to blast off!

Glen tried to peer into the coin slot, but the machine wouldn't stand still. A crowd of kids had gathered to watch, as smoke started to pour out of the top.

"It's going to explode!" one of the kids yelled.

Then, suddenly, all the pinball lights popped off. The metal balls stopped rolling. The bells and buzzers wheezed into silence. And, from the bottom of the machine, Mac dropped to the floor.

As Scott started to reach for Mac, a big hairy hand clamped down on his shoulder. Hard. It was Big Bruno.

"What's going on here?" he boomed. Then he glanced down and spotted Mac. Mac's claws were wedged in the wooden floor. He was struggling to free himself.

Big Bruno squinted. Scott could tell he wasn't exactly sure what he was looking at.

Bruno lifted his face and shoved it inches away from Scott's nose. His hot, stinking breath filled Scott's nostrils as he roared, "No pets allowed!"

Then he lifted his huge foot.

Scott glanced at Mac. He was twisting and turning. Frantically trying to free himself from the wooden planks.

Scott watched in horror as Bruno brought his black boot down.

Down.

Down on Mac.

To grind him into the floor—forever.

13

Scott shot out his hands and plowed right into Big Bruno. The manager stumbled backward, trying to keep his balance.

Glen quickly scooped Mac up from the floor. "Got him!" he yelled to Scott. He stuffed Mac into his jacket pocket. Then the two boys ran.

As they raced out of the arcade, they could hear Big Bruno hit the floor with a huge thud.

"Guess we can't go back there again!" Scott shouted as they dashed to the bus stop.

"That's for sure," Glen replied, panting.

Scott couldn't stop trembling on the bus ride home. He didn't feel much like talking, and Glen didn't either.

"What are we going to do with Mac now?" Scott finally asked when they were safely back in his room.

"What can we do?" Glen shrugged. "I think we're stuck with him."

"Well, from now on he's staying in his aquarium," Scott said firmly. "And we'll definitely have to make a cover for it."

Glen reached into his pocket and pulled Mac out.

"What happened to him?" Glen cried. "He looks horrible!"

He really does, Scott thought. Mac was all shriveled up. And wrinkled—like a prune. He had shrunk to the size of a tiny bug.

Scott stared at his face. His eyes were sunken in. And his lips were cracked and curled back so that his jagged teeth jutted out. He resembled a dry sponge with baby fangs.

His little chest heaved up and down. And he was wheezing. Gasping for breath. Scott couldn't help feeling sorry for him. He took him from Glen and gently slid him inside his aquarium.

Then, the instant Mac hit the water, it happened.

Mac started to change.

Into something no one—not even the kids who lived on Fear Street—would believe.

14

"**N**ooooo!" Glen shouted.

Scott practically knocked the aquarium over as he leaped back. "No way!" he gasped.

Mac was transforming.

He was growing darker. Because the hair all over his body was growing longer and thicker.

His arms started to bulge, getting bigger and stronger. His legs throbbed as they grew, too.

Even the tiny little wings on Mac's back began to expand—looking more and more like the wings on the monkeys from *The Wizard of Oz.*

When Mac finally stopped growing, he was

bigger than a hamster. Much bigger. Now he was about the size of a rabbit.

"What if he keeps growing?" Glen asked. "What if he grows as big as a real monkey? Or even a gorilla?"

"That's not going to happen," Scott said, trying to convince himself as well as Glen. "But I'll tell you one thing. I sure don't want him running around loose in my room."

"I don't blame you," Glen replied.

Scott pulled a huge dictionary off his bookshelf and placed it down on top of the aquarium. He slid it over slightly to leave a sliver of space for fresh air to enter. "That should hold him," he declared.

"Uh-oh," Glen said.

"What?" Scott shot a frightened glance at Mac.

"Look what time it is!" Glen said. "If I don't get home right now, my mother will have a fit." Glen headed for the door.

Scott followed him down the stairs. As they reached the landing, they spotted Kelly. She was twirling around the living room in a poofy pink dress, pretending to be a model or something.

"My mother's making her a dress for that

stupid school dance she's going to," Scott whispered to Glen.

That's all his mother had been talking about lately. Kelly's first dance. Kelly's first dance. His mom made a big deal about first anythings, like Scott's first home run. But that was okay, Scott thought. *That* was important.

"Like anybody is gonna dance with her," Glen interrupted his thoughts.

"Yeah, really."

"I'll see you later, Mrs. Adams," Glen called to Scott's mom as he headed out the door.

"Be careful going home." She didn't glance up. She was struggling to pin the bottom of Kelly's dress while Kelly swished around. "Stay still, Kelly," she ordered.

Kelly stopped swishing—and started twirling. She twirled her long blond hair into a bun on top of her head. "How do you think I should wear my hair?" she asked. "Like this, Mom? Or like this?" she asked, twirling it into yet another style.

"I think you should wear it down. You have such beautiful hair. It would be a shame not to show it off," Mom said.

"Oh, puke," Scott muttered as he headed back through the living room.

"Shut up," Kelly snapped back. "You immature little twerp!"

Immature. Scott hated it more than anything when Kelly called him immature. She was only a year older than he was. One lousy year. But she was always treating him like she was a grown-up and he was a baby.

"Witch," he screamed at her.

"Scott," his mother scolded. "Enough!" She stuck one more pin in Kelly's dress. "Okay. I'm finished. Go upstairs and change," she told Kelly.

"You always take her side," Scott complained to his mother.

For a minute she looked as though she was going to explode. But she didn't. "Look," she said calmly. "I know I've been paying lots of attention to Kelly lately. But this dance is really important to her. And if she doesn't have the dress she saw in the mall, she's going to make everybody's life miserable."

That was the truth. Kelly had dragged their mother to the mall a million times, trying to find the perfect dress. And they had finally found it. But their mom refused to buy it. She said it cost practically as much as a new car. So she decided to try to make it.

The timer on the stove in the kitchen went off. "Oh, shoot," his mother said as she jumped up off the couch. "I almost forgot about dinner." She headed for the kitchen.

Scott charged up the stairs, taking them two at a time—before his mom had a chance to ask him to set the table or something.

"Kelly thinks she's so cool, 'cause she's going to some stupid dance. In some stupid dress," Scott muttered as he entered his room.

He walked over to his dresser mirror and started imitating Kelly, using his best bratty-sounding Kelly voice. "Which way should I wear my hair?" Scott tried twirling the hair on top of his head the same way Kelly had. "This way?" He made a face at himself in the mirror. "Or this way?"

He would have gone on complaining, but something in the mirror caught his eye. Something that reminded him that he had bigger things to worry about than Kelly.

The dictionary on top of Mac's aquarium was gone.

15

Scott's eyes darted around the room.

There it was.

The dictionary.

Pages open and rumpled. On the floor.

Scott picked it up and placed it back on top of the aquarium. "I don't believe this," he mumbled to himself.

Then he reached for the thickest volume of his encyclopedia and stacked it on top of the dictionary. He made the small opening for air even tinier.

Mac will have to be a magician to get out now, Scott thought.

Scott walked backward to his bed. He didn't want to take his eyes off the aqua ape.

He propped himself up against the headboard and stared at Mac. When his mom called him for dinner, he told her he wasn't feeling well. Upset stomach, he said. There was no way he was leaving this room—not until he was sure Mac couldn't escape.

Scott decided to stay awake all night and check Mac's tank every fifteen minutes. Even if he had to use toothpicks to keep his eyelids open to do it.

Every time Scott got up and peered into the tank, Mac waved at him. The aqua ape looked harmless. But Scott wasn't taking any chances.

He glanced at the clock on his nightstand. It was 11:45. At midnight Scott would get up to check on Mac again. But he was growing sleepy. Very sleepy.

He didn't feel really safe all alone with the aqua ape. He thought about all the trouble Mac had caused at the mall. That was pretty weird. Then he remembered how Mac had suddenly sprouted all that hair—and had grown twice as big, right before his eyes. That was *really* weird.

When Scott checked the clock again, it was well past midnight. I fell asleep, Scott thought as he shot up in bed. But he didn't go check on Mac. He didn't even glance at the aquarium.

Scott threw on his clothes and sneaked out of the house. He was headed for Fear Lake. He didn't want to go. But he couldn't seem to stop himself. It was as if the lake were somehow calling to him, somehow controlling his every move, his every thought.

He walked through the woods as if he were in a trance. It was dark. And silent. Totally silent.

This is too scary, he thought. *No one should be out here. In the middle of the night. Alone.*

He tried to turn back. But every path he took seemed totally unfamiliar to him. And all of them led to the same place. All of them led to Fear Lake.

"You have the power to create life!" The words echoed through the darkness as Scott found himself moving closer and closer to the lake.

Was he imagining the voice? Was it simply echoing in his own mind? Scott couldn't be certain. But he was sure of one thing—he did not have the power to turn back. Something was forcing him to continue onward.

Then, suddenly, without warning, the entire sky lit up with lightning. And the sound of thunder roared above him.

"You have the power to create life!" There was the voice again. Only this time it was much louder. And seemed to be coming from . . . the lake!

Scott whirled. To head back. But the invisible force turned him around. And propelled him forward. He felt as if someone—or something— were pushing him from behind.

"Stop!" Scott screamed. "Stop!" But the louder he yelled the faster he was shoved toward the lake.

Faster. Faster. He was sure he was going to be pushed right into the dark water.

But just as he reached the water's edge, the force stopped pushing.

Scott stood still. Trying to catch his breath. That's when he noticed the water in Fear Lake. It was bubbling and churning—the same way the water had bubbled and churned in Mac's bowl.

And then it happened.

A huge monster rose from the inky water directly in front of Scott.

Scott thought about closing his eyes. Closing his eyes tightly so he wouldn't have to look at the monster. But he was afraid that if he did that the monster would grab him and pull him down. Down into the evil water.

So he forced himself to stare at the creature. And his heart nearly burst in his chest—the monster looked just like Mac! It *was* Mac. Only worse.

It was dark and hairy and huge, with giant wings on its back. And its teeth were pointy—as sharp as sharks' teeth.

Scott could hear screams in the distance. They sounded familiar. Scott hoped it was someone coming to rescue him.

Mac reached down and grabbed Scott around the neck with one huge, slimy, hairy paw. He yanked Scott six feet off the ground.

Scott tried to struggle free. But it was hopeless. This monster-Mac was stronger than twelve weight lifters.

Scott opened his mouth to yell, but the monster swatted his other huge paw over Scott's lips, nearly knocking his head off.

The screams in the distance grew louder.

Closer.

But if someone *was* out there—trying to save him—it was too late.

Because Scott knew there was no way anyone could help.

There was no way he would ever escape Mac.

16

Mac suddenly released his grip.

Scott crashed to the ground. Hard.

His eyes popped wide open.

It took him a minute to realize that he wasn't lying in the mud by the side of Fear Lake. He was lying on the floor. In his bedroom. He had tossed and turned himself right out of the bed.

Just a dream, thought Scott. Just a horrible dream.

Scott closed his eyes. But they flew wide open when he heard the scream.

A high scream.

Kelly's screams—the screams he had heard

echoing in his dream. Only he wasn't dreaming anymore.

Scott saw his parents race past his door. "What's going on?" he called.

"I don't know," his mother answered, without stopping.

Scott scrambled to his feet. But just as he was about to dash after her, he spotted something terrifying. And he wished he were still dreaming.

There on the floor lay the dictionary and the encyclopedia.

Please, oh please, let Mac be in there, Scott prayed as he cautiously approached the aquarium.

But Mac was gone.

Scott rushed out of his room and down the hall. As he reached the door to Kelly's bedroom, he half expected to see Mac standing six feet tall, looming over her.

Scott didn't see Mac. But he was pretty sure Mac was responsible for what he *did* see.

Kelly stood at the foot of her bed. Her long blond hair was twisted together in front of her face and tied in a million little knots. Scott could barely even see the tip of her nose sticking out.

"How on earth did this happen?" Scott's

father asked, trying to untie some of the hair in front of her face.

"I don't know!" Kelly answered hysterically. "I just woke up like this!"

Scott knew he had to find Mac before anyone else did. He glanced around Kelly's room, checking the floor, the curtains, the desk. Then he spotted Mac crawling out from under Kelly's pillow.

Scott slid past his parents and sat down on Kelly's bed, right in front of Mac. To hide him.

"Oooooouch!" Kelly screamed. "You're hurting me!"

"I hate to tell you this, Kel," their mother said apologetically. "I think we're going to have to cut it."

"Noooooo!" Kelly screamed and burst into tears.

Scott felt like screaming, too—when he saw Mac clap his hands with joy. Then the little ape leaped off the bed and darted across the floor—in plain view.

"Maybe you should go down in the kitchen and put some peanut butter in Kelly's hair," Scott blurted out. He had to get everyone out of there—fast.

Kelly cried harder and his mother frowned at

him. "Really," Scott said. "Glen got some gum in his hair once and that's how his mom got it out." No one bothered to answer.

Mac stood between Kelly's bare feet, grinning up at Scott.

"I promise you, it'll grow back," their mother said, trying to comfort Kelly.

Scott picked up one of the stuffed animals on Kelly's bed and hurled it at Mac. He missed. Mac waved at him.

"Leave my stuff alone!" Kelly wailed.

Scott's father glanced at him with angry, narrowed eyes.

"I can't even begin to imagine how this happened," Scott's father began, trying to break the tension. "What were you doing? Having a wrestling match in your sleep?" he asked. He was trying to make Kelly smile. It wasn't working.

Scott gasped as Mac strutted toward his father's pajama leg.

"What?" Scott's father asked.

"Nothing," Scott lied. He watched Mac crawl closer to his dad. "I just can't believe that Kelly's got to get her hair cut off, that's all."

"Drop dead!" Kelly screamed. Then she shoved Scott off the bed.

This was his chance.

His only chance.

Scott fell to the floor. He sprawled out at his father's feet and stretched his hand out to grab Mac.

His eyes met Mac's for a moment.

Scott swore Mac winked at him. Then he scampered to the wall and slithered right down one of the large, open air vents.

Oh, no, Scott thought. *Mac is running loose in the house—and I don't know what he'll do next. He's out of control!*

17

"**H**e's running loose in my house!" Scott told Glen for the hundredth time. "We've got to get him out of there!"

Scott turned his bicycle into his driveway and hurried into the garage. Glen was right behind him.

All day at school Scott had asked himself the same question over and over: What is Mac doing now?

"I can't believe you didn't tell your mom about Mac," Glen said, parking his bike.

"Do you know what kind of trouble I'd be in if she knew about Mac?"

"Yeah." Glen nodded. "But what if she saw Mac running around the house today? Or what if he did something even worse? Just think how really mad she'll be. What are you going to say then?"

"We're going to play dumb," he told Glen. "If something bad has happened, let me do all the talking."

"Let's start looking for Mac in the den," Scott suggested. "That's where the air vents in Kelly's room lead to."

Scott turned the doorknob to the den. He hesitated for a moment. Okay, he thought. Now I'm ready—for anything.

But he wasn't ready for what he saw when he opened the door. Kelly stood in the den. Her hair was cut shorter than he'd ever seen it. It was almost as short as his hair.

"Doesn't Kelly's hair look nice?" his mother asked in a tone of voice that told Scott the only acceptable answer was *yes.*

But Scott couldn't speak.

Glen picked up the slack. "Nice hairdo, Kelly."

"Yeah. Nice hairdo, Kel," Scott repeated.

That seemed to satisfy Scott's mother. "See," she said to Kelly. "Didn't I tell you?"

Then she turned her attention back to Scott. "Kelly and I are going out for a few minutes," she told him. "We have to go to the fabric store to pick up a little more material for Kelly's dress. We shouldn't be too long. Please behave while I'm gone." She always said that last part before she left the house.

"Okay," Scott answered. He couldn't wait for his mother to leave. He needed time to search for Mac.

When Scott's mother opened the door, she hesitated. "It looks like it's going to rain," she said. "Maybe we shouldn't go now."

"Mom," Kelly whined. "We have to go. Puh-lease."

"Okay, okay," their mom gave in.

Kelly turned back to them before she stepped into the hall. "My dress is on the couch," she said. "Don't you dare touch it while we're gone." Then she slammed the door behind her.

Glen crossed over to the couch and touched the dress. "There. I touched it," he said.

"It doesn't seem like my mom knows anything about Mac," Scott said, relieved.

"If you're lucky, she'll never find out," Glen replied. "At least he hasn't done anything bad since this morning."

"We've got about an hour before my mom gets back. We've *got* to find him." Scott headed out of the den. "Let's start with my room."

As they passed the kitchen, Scott heard a noise. A loud, crunching noise. Glen heard it, too.

"What is that?" Glen asked.

"I don't know." Scott walked slowly into the kitchen toward the sound. It came from one of the cabinets.

Crunch. Crunch. Crunch.

"What is that?" Glen repeated.

"There's only one way to find out," Scott answered. He reached out and grabbed one of the cabinet handles.

He really didn't want to open it.

He knew that there was trouble behind that door. Big trouble that started with the letter *M!*

But he had no choice.

He had to open that door.

18

Scott slowly swung the cabinet door open.

And Mac tumbled out—in an avalanche of cereal, pasta, beans, sugar, and flour.

"Look what he did!" Scott cried.

Every box in the cabinet had been clawed to shreds. And half-eaten food littered the cabinet everywhere—chewed-up cookies, gnawed macaroni, crunched Cruncho-Crispies—Kelly's favorite cereal—nibbled lima beans, chomped crackers, munched potato chips.

"He opened every single box and tasted everything," Glen noted. "Except the prunes."

It was true. The box of prunes remained untouched on the cabinet shelf.

Scott glanced around the kitchen. The food had tumbled out of the cabinet, onto the counter, and had spilled onto the floor.

And there was Mac. Standing in the middle of it. Covered in flour. He looked like the Abominable Snowman.

As he stomped around the crumbs, picking out cracker pieces, little clouds of flour puffed from his furry body.

"My mom's going to go crazy when she sees this!"

"Don't worry," Glen told him. "We'll clean it up before she gets home."

Scott hoped they would have time to do that. But first he had to figure out a way to get Mac under control. And he didn't have a lot of time to think about it.

There was only one thing for Scott to do. He was going to have to grab Mac quickly and find something to put him in. Something with a lid.

Scott knew that he had to move fast. He couldn't give Mac time to escape again. So, without any warning, Scott dove right at Mac, sliding on some flour and rice.

But, as usual, Mac was quicker than Scott. In

fact he was so quick it took Scott a minute to realize that he didn't have Mac in his grip.

"Get him, Glen!" Scott shouted as Mac tore across the kitchen floor.

Glen lunged for Mac. Only Mac was way too fast for Glen. He dodged him. And Glen went sailing across the floor right smack into one of the legs of the kitchen table. Head first.

"Oooooouch!" Glen moaned. "I think I broke my head!"

"You did not break your head," Scott groaned.

"Yeah, well it sure feels like it," Glen shot back, rubbing his forehead. "My whole head is pounding."

"If we don't catch Mac and clean this place up before my mother gets home, it's going to be pounding even more," Scott said as he pulled Glen to his feet. "Because she's going to be screaming at us at the top of her lungs."

Glen bolted out of the kitchen. "Come on," he shouted. "If Mac ran straight when he left the kitchen, he should be in your father's study."

Scott nearly choked at the sight in his father's study. Glen was right. Mac was in his father's study. Or at least he had been.

Papers and files and books covered the floor. The old-fashioned inkwell his father kept in the center of the desk had been knocked over. And ink was dripping all over his father's fancy leather blotter.

"Your mother's not going to be the only one screaming at the top of her lungs," Glen said as he stood staring at the mess.

"Tell me about it." Scott's heart sank. He knew that there was no way in the world they would be able to clean up his father's study and the kitchen before his mother returned home.

"Wh-what are we going to do?" Glen stammered.

"First we have to find Mac," Scott answered. "And we'd better find him fast—before he destroys the whole house!"

Scott took off down the hallway, with Glen right behind him. If Mac was still moving in a straight line, he was probably headed for the one room that was off-limits to everyone—the dining room!

"Hurry up," Scott urged Glen. All of his mother's expensive china and crystal were displayed in the dining room. And if something happened to any of her "good stuff," his mother would kill him. It was as simple as that.

Scott rushed into the dining room and glanced around frantically.

It took him a minute to realize that everything was okay.

Nothing was broken.

Mac hadn't been in the room.

"At least he's not in here," Scott said, feeling incredibly relieved.

Only he wasn't relieved for long.

When he left the dining room and headed into the den, he saw something so horrifying that he wished Mac had broken all of his mother's fine crystal instead.

A pile of smashed crystal would have been a whole lot easier for his mother to forgive.

19

Kelly's dress. The dress for the dance.

The one that Scott's mother had been working so hard on for weeks . . . was ruined.

Scott covered his face. He couldn't stand to look at what Mac had done.

Both sleeves had been torn off. One of them was on the floor, ripped to shreds. The other was stuck to the side of the couch with pins.

There were gold beads tossed all over the room. But there wasn't a single one on Kelly's dress anymore. It had taken his mother days to sew on all those beads!

Worst of all, horrible stains covered almost

every inch of the material. Stains that looked like they had come from a thick black marker.

"Your mom is going to go ballistic if she sees this!" Glen shrieked.

"Yeah." Scott uncovered his face and stared, dumbfounded, at the disaster. "And she's going to blame us."

"Not if we fix it before she gets home. That's what we'll do. We'll fix it. You'll see. Everything will be okay. We'll fix everything." Glen ran around the room trying to collect all the beads.

Scott slowly walked over to the couch and peered down at the remains of Kelly's dress.

It wasn't going to be okay. And Scott knew it. There was no way in the world the two of them could ever fix what Mac had done now.

"It's no use, Glen," Scott said numbly, too shocked to panic. "There's nothing we can do."

Then Scott spotted Mac—climbing up the side of the curtains behind the couch. "There he is!" Scott screamed.

Mac scurried up the curtains and ran across the top of the curtain rod before Scott could grab him.

"Mac!" Scott screamed. "Get back here!"

But Mac jumped off the top of the curtain rod and tore across the room.

Glen tore after him. And so did Scott.

"Stay with him!" Scott ordered Glen as they chased Mac down the hallway and back toward the kitchen. "If we lose him again, who knows what he'll do!"

"He's too fast." Glen panted. "We're never going to catch him!"

Then Scott had a brilliant idea. If they couldn't catch Mac, maybe they could just chase him right out of the house.

"Glen," Scott called as they ran through the kitchen and into the hallway. "Forget about Mac, and go open the door in the den that leads out to the garage."

"Why?" Glen asked.

"Because I'm going to try to chase Mac right out into the garage. Then we can get rid of him," Scott whispered. "Forever!"

"Good thinking!" Glen trotted toward the den, while Scott raced after Mac.

Mac led Scott through every room on the first floor of the house. Finally the furry creature darted back into the den.

"Get away from the door!" Scott screamed as he chased Mac across the room. "You'll scare him and he'll run the other way!"

90

Glen quickly jumped aside. And Mac dashed through the open door, just the way Scott hoped he would.

"Come on!" Scott yelled. "I'll chase him outside. You get ready to hit the switch that closes the garage door."

Scott and Glen darted out the den door and slammed it behind them—just as a bucket of nuts and bolts crashed down from a shelf that ran along the left side of the garage wall.

Scott peered up and spotted Mac zipping across the shelf.

"Oh, no!" Scott gasped as Mac stopped to push a can of paint off the shelf. As it hit the floor, the lid blew off.

Splat!

Red paint flew everywhere—the walls, the floor, the workbench. And worst of all, a big blotch splashed across the side of Scott's father's white car.

Scott stared at the car, horrified. "Why couldn't Dad have been driving the car pool today?" he moaned.

"If your father sees this, we're dead meat."

Mac jumped down from the shelf and landed on top of the car.

"You're going to be the dead one!" Scott screamed at Mac. Then he lunged for the hood of the car. But Mac escaped once more.

Only this time Scott was happy. Because this time Mac ran straight out of the garage. And straight down the driveway.

"Close the door!" Scott yelled at Glen. "Close the door!"

Glen hit the button on the side of the wall that controlled the automatic garage door.

And as the door started to move down, Mac turned around and started running back up the driveway.

"Hurry up! Hurry up!" Scott jumped up and down and hollered at the door, as if that would make it move faster.

He held his breath as the door came down. Closer and closer to the floor.

The door was only inches away from the floor now.

Mac was only inches away from being gone forever.

We did it! Scott thought. *We did it!*

And then Scott heard the cry.

A terrifying cry.

20

"**W**e squashed him!" Glen screamed.

Scott could see that for himself. Poking out from under the closed garage door were one of Mac's arms and one of his legs. And they weren't moving. The rest of Mac had to be smashed under the door.

Scott felt sick to his stomach. He never really wanted to kill the creature. He just wanted to get rid of it.

Scott hit the button to make the door go back up again. Outside, a fine drizzle had begun to fall.

Well, he thought. It doesn't look as though Mac is going to be a problem for us anymore.

Scott moved closer to take a better look. Mac's head was almost flat. His body was surrounded by a puddle of slime. Little raindrops splattered in the goo.

"He's totally smushed," Scott announced.

"Too gross," Glen said.

"Yeah," Scott agreed, peering down at Mac. "We probably ought to bury him or something," he said to Glen.

Glen nodded. "We're going to have to scrape him off the floor first," he pointed out. He nudged Mac with the tip of his sneaker—and one of Mac's legs fell off.

"Oh, gross!" Scott shouted. He turned his head away.

"Come on. We'd better move fast," Glen said. "It's starting to rain hard now."

Mac was getting wet. Raindrops bounced off his squished head, his pancake body, his crushed arms and legs.

But now . . . he seemed to be . . . changing.

He wasn't so flat anymore.

He seemed to be puffing up.

"Oh, no," Scott gasped. "Not again!"

94

21

"The water is bringing him back to life!" Scott screamed.

"And look at his leg!" Glen cried. "It's growing back!"

"That's impossible," Scott shouted. But as he bent closer, he realized Glen was right. Mac's leg was growing back.

A piece of jagged bone stuck out from the place where Mac's leg should have been. And it was growing longer and longer. Then strands of muscles and veins sprouted around the bone.

Scott noticed that the old leg, the one that had fallen off, was shriveling up as fast as the new one grew. "This is the creepiest thing I've ever seen," Scott said, backing away from Mac.

"How can this be happening?" Glen backed away from Mac, too.

"It must be the water," Scott answered. "Remember when we came home from the arcade and he was all shriveled up? Once we placed him back in the water he was fine. Better than fine. It made him grow. It looks like water can cure Mac of anything!"

"Yeah," Glen gasped. "Even death!"

Scott watched in horror as Mac jumped to his feet, looking as big as before—and stronger than ever!

We're never going to get rid of Mac! Scott realized. *Never! He's totally indestructible!*

"What are we going to do now?" Glen asked in a nervous little whisper.

Mac stood there, with his eyes glued to the two of them.

Scott's mind raced. He had no idea what to do.

"Maybe if we just leave him alone out here, he'll go away," Glen suggested hopefully.

Scott thought about that for a second. He wished with all his heart that Mac would just go away. But that wasn't going to happen. And Scott knew it.

There was only one thing to do. Somehow, someway, they had to catch Mac and keep him locked up forever.

Without a word Scott started inching toward Mac.

Mac didn't move.

"What are you doing?" Glen asked.

"Just shut up," Scott told Glen. He took another step toward Mac.

Mac still didn't move.

"I'm not going to hurt you, Mac," Scott said in a gentle tone. He didn't want Mac to tear off again. "I just want to pet you," Scott lied. "That's all."

"Are you crazy, or what?" Glen asked in disbelief.

Scott reached out to snatch Mac. Mac screeched in fury, and swiped at Scott's face with his sharp claws.

Scott jerked his head back, but Mac dug his claws right into the top of Scott's hand. "Ow!" Scott screamed.

Mac screeched again. Then he leaped from Scott's hand onto one of the shelves in the garage.

As Scott cradled his hand, Mac picked up a

hammer and sent it hurling right for Scott's head.

"Look out!" Glen screamed.

Scott ducked just in time. The hammer missed his head by an inch.

Then Mac picked up a screwdriver and threw it—like a spear—at Glen.

"He's trying to kill us!" Glen screamed. He barely escaped being hit. "Let's get inside!"

They both ran for the door.

"Hurry up!" Scott yelled as Glen struggled with the doorknob. "Hurry up!"

Glen finally pushed the door open, and he and Scott rushed into the den.

Scott tried to slam the door behind them. But it wouldn't shut.

Because Mac was pushing on it from the other side.

"Help me, Glen!" Scott called. He pushed the door with all his might.

Glen threw his weight against the door, too.

But Mac was stronger than both of them combined. Scott and Glen fell on their backs as Mac burst through the door, tore through the den, and disappeared into the house.

22

"Come on." Scott jumped to his feet. "We have to call the police."

"And tell them what?" Glen demanded. "That we've got a giant killer aqua ape running loose in the house? Like they're really going to believe that."

"So we'll tell them that a burglar broke in or a wild animal or something. Anything to get them over here," Scott answered.

"They aren't—" Glen began.

"Mac thinks we tried to crush him with the garage door," Scott interrupted. "He's mad—

and he's going to come after us. I'm calling 9-1-1 right now."

Scott and Glen rushed to the kitchen phone. Scott started to dial. And then he heard the screams coming from the den.

"Scott!" The sound of his mother's voice was almost more terrifying than anything Mac had done. "You get in here right this second!"

Scott's stomach clenched. Now he felt really sick. As he and Glen trudged into the den, Scott's mind raced to find a way to tell his mother about Mac.

"What have you done!" Scott's mother shrieked at him the moment he stepped into the room.

"Mom, I didn't do it," Scott said. "I swear I didn't."

Scott's mother glared at him as she stood holding the shreds of Kelly's dress. "Then who did?"

"We grew an aqua ape," Scott blurted out. "He got way bigger than the instructions said. Now he's loose in the house. He's destroying everything. And he's after me and Glen! You've got to help us."

"Oh, Scott." His mother shook her head in

disgust. "Do you really expect me to believe that story?"

"Mom, please," Scott begged. "I'm telling the truth. Right, Glen?"

Glen nodded his head, looking terrified.

"I don't want to hear one more word of this nonsense," Scott's mother yelled. She was angrier than Scott had ever seen her. She threw the ruined dress onto the couch.

"I hate you!" Kelly screamed at Scott. "I hate you both!" Then she burst into tears.

"Don't cry, Kelly," her mother said soothingly. She gently stroked Kelly's hair—well, what was left of it—as she glared at Scott. "It's okay."

"It's not okay!" Kelly wailed. "My dress is ruined! Now I can't go to the dance!"

"We're just going to have to go out and buy the dress in the mall," her mother said. "And you, young man, are going to pay for it," she said to Scott. "Out of your allowance. Even if it takes the rest of your life!"

Scott stood silent.

"In fact," his mother continued, "Kelly and I are going to go out right now to get it. I will deal with you and this mess when I get back!"

Scott's mother and Kelly left without another word.

"I wish I'd never heard of aqua apes," Scott moaned. Then his head dropped to his chest—and Mac sprang out from between the sofa cushions.

"There he is!" Glen screamed. Mac screamed back even louder, baring his teeth.

"Get him," Scott yelled.

Mac grabbed a handful of the beads from Kelly's ruined dress and hurled them at Scott and Glen.

Three of the beads hit Scott in the face. *"Ye-ouch!"* Scott cried, trying to rub away the stinging pain.

Mac grabbed one of the sleeves of Kelly's dress and raced out of the den.

"We've got to find him," Scott said. "He's not going to stop until he gets us."

"Let's split up," Glen suggested. "You take the upstairs. I'll look for him down here."

"Good idea!" Scott agreed.

Scott charged up the stairs. The first door he came to was the hall linen closet. He peeked inside. No Mac hiding in the bedsheets. He bent down on his hands and knees to check the closet floor—when someone tapped him on the shoulder.

Scott sprang up and screamed.

"It's just me," Glen whispered.

"What are you doing here? You're supposed to be checking the downstairs."

"I—uh—decided we shouldn't split up after all," Glen stammered. "It's, um, not safe. . . ."

"Sshh!" Scott interrupted. "Listen." Scott stared into the closet, expecting to see Mac jump out at them.

Then he realized the sound he heard wasn't coming from the closet. It was coming from down the hall.

"It sounds like water running," Glen said.

"Come on!" Scott grabbed Glen and tugged him down the hall. "He's in the bathroom!"

The moment they reached the bathroom door, Scott gasped. Water was spilling over the sink, flooding the bathroom floor.

"Look at this! The whole place is soaked!" Scott quickly turned the water off. "Get some towels!"

Glen jerked a cabinet open, yanked out some towels, and threw them down on the floor.

As Scott and Glen soaked up the water, they noticed even more water pouring out onto the floor.

Only it wasn't coming from the sink.

It was coming from under the lid of the toilet bowl.

"What is going on?" Scott lifted the lid of the toilet to peer inside.

And there was Mac.

Glaring up at him.

His eyes were jet-black now. The centers were red and glowing.

Mac bared his ugly teeth. They were longer and sharper than ever. Even his fur looked sharp, like porcupine quills.

Scott slammed the toilet shut. "He's in there. And he's bigger and meaner than ever!"

"Flush him!" Glen screamed. "Flush him!" He sat down on the top part of the lid. "Hurry up!"

Mac shoved hard against the lid. The lid flew open with a bang. Glen crashed to the floor.

"Get up!" Scott screamed, trying to hold the lid down by himself. "Help me!"

Glen jumped up and sat on the lid again. But Mac snapped it open—just enough to shoot out a furry claw. And jab it into Glen's leg.

"Oooow," Glen wailed, grasping his thigh.

"Stand up a little so I can shove his hand back inside," Scott cried.

Glen stood up and Scott tried to push Mac's

hand down into the toilet, but Mac swiped at Scott's arm. Scott let out a shriek as blood trickled from the cut.

Now both of Mac's arms were hanging out of the toilet. Then he popped his head out, too. He was grinning. An evil grin.

Scott leaned over, picked up the toilet bowl brush next to the sink, and batted Mac with it.

The hairy creature slid from the rim and plopped into the water.

Glen slammed the lid down once again. The two boys leaped on top of it together.

"Flush it!" Glen screamed. "Flush it! Now!"

Scott reached behind him and pushed the handle down hard.

From inside, they heard Mac screech—long and loud.

Scott froze as he heard the water swirling around the inside of the bowl.

Then he heard the sound of the water being sucked down through the pipes.

Then everything went silent.

23

"**Y**ou look."

"I don't want to look," Glen said. "Why do we have to look, anyway?"

"We have to make sure he's really gone. That's why." Scott sighed.

"Well, it's your toilet bowl, so you look."

It took all the courage Scott had to lift the toilet lid and peek inside.

He lifted it slowly.

He stared into the water.

There was no sign of Mac. One flush had sent Mac swirling out of their lives for good. As Scott closed the lid, another sigh escaped his lips—this one a sigh of relief.

Scott glanced around the bathroom. "We'd better start cleaning up this mess before my mother gets home. Go downstairs to the kitchen and get a mop so we can sop up all this water from the floor."

Glen headed out.

Scott lifted the soaking wet bath mat off the floor and dropped it into the bathtub. He sat on the edge of the tub and started wringing what seemed like gallons of water out of the mat.

Crack! The lid of the toilet blew open!

24

Scott watched in horror as Mac burst out of the toilet and flew straight at him.

Scott screamed as Mac hovered above him.

Mac had the wingspan of a bat now. He flapped his wings wildly and let out a bloodcurdling shriek.

Scott couldn't take his eyes off Mac's glistening yellow teeth. They had grown to the size of fangs.

Mac dove down, claws stretched out at Scott.

"Get away from me!" Scott covered his face with one arm.

Mac retreated. Then he swooped down again, his mouth open wide—ready to bite.

Scott dashed out of the bathroom. He ran down the hallway. Mac flew after him. Screeching and swooping.

"Glen!" Scott screamed as he reached the top of the stairs. "Help me!" Scott barely got the words out of his mouth before Mac attacked, diving straight for his face.

Scott felt Mac's razor-sharp claws scratch his cheek. Scott jerked away. His feet slipped on the carpeted stairs. Slipped out from under him. And he tumbled down the stairs.

When he reached the bottom, he scrambled up—before Mac could swoop down on him again.

He raced through the living room toward the kitchen. Mac hovered right over him. Screeching and diving.

Glen headed out of the kitchen with a mop in one hand and a cookie in the other. At the sight of Mac, he dropped both. "Where did he come from?" he screamed, dashing back into the kitchen.

"He came back out of the toilet!" Scott yelled. "And now he's trying to kill me!"

Mac swooped down at Scott's face again. This time, Scott tried to grab him. But Mac's fur jabbed into Scott's palms. "Don't touch him!" Scott told Glen. "His hair feels like needles!"

"I don't want to touch him!" Glen hollered as he dove under the kitchen table.

Scott's eyes darted around the kitchen—searching for something he could use for protection. He thought about grabbing the flyswatter, but no way would that stop Mac.

Mac swooped under the table and headed for Glen. "Watch out!" Scott screamed. Glen rolled out of the way before Mac could claw him.

Mac circled the kitchen and landed on top of the refrigerator. And for a minute he just perched there—cackling at Scott and Glen.

"We've got to do something!" Glen cried. "Or we're going to die!"

Scott noticed the frying pan sitting on top of the stove. It gave him an idea.

With one eye on Mac, Scott edged over to the stove and grabbed the pan. He hid it behind his back.

"Come on, you stupid pig-monkey," Scott called angrily. "Come and get me!"

"Are you out of your mind!" Glen jumped to the other side of the room.

"Come on, Mac!" Scott yelled again, ignoring Glen. "Come get me, you dumb aqua ape!"

Mac fluttered his wings. He bared his teeth. He let out one, loud, angry screech. And then he dove from the top of the refrigerator—straight at Scott.

Scott swung the frying pan and prepared to slam Mac the same way he would a fast ball. Just as Mac came about an arm's length away, Scott swung as hard as he could. A direct hit!

Mac sailed across the kitchen and slammed into the opposite wall with a splat. Then he crumpled to the floor, stunned.

"We've got to put him in something quick—before he wakes up," Scott told Glen.

"Then what are we going to do with him?" Glen asked. He bent down and started digging through one of the lower cabinets.

"Nothing. You know how he gets all dry and wrinkly when he's out of the water too long?"

"Yeah," Glen answered, moving on to the next cabinet.

"Well, I bet if we keep him trapped out of water, he'll dry up completely. He'll turn back into one of the crystals."

"Maybe," Glen answered. He didn't sound convinced.

Scott noticed the cookie jar on the counter. "We'll put him in this," he said as he grabbed the jar.

Mac started to moan.

"Hurry up! Hurry up!" Glen warned.

Scott quickly opened the jar and dumped all the cookies out onto the counter. Then he tiptoed over to Mac. "Just pick him up and put him in here," Scott whispered to Glen.

"I'm not picking him up," Glen said.

"I smashed him," Scott insisted. "You pick him up!"

"I'm not touching him!" Glen screamed.

"Fine." Scott grabbed the aqua ape by the tip of one wing and dropped him in the jar.

"Now what?" Glen asked.

"Tape!" Scott answered. He grabbed a roll of heavy-duty tape from the junk drawer. "Hold the lid on," Scott ordered. Then he used the whole roll to tape the top on the jar.

"I'm going to get some more tape," Scott announced. "Just to make sure."

"Well, hurry up!" Glen screamed after him. "Before he wakes up and chews through this thing."

Scott dashed out to the garage and came back

with a roll of clear tape, a roll of electrical tape, and two rolls of masking tape.

"I thought I heard him scratching around in there," Glen said. "He's waking up."

Scott and Glen wrapped the entire cookie jar in tape. They didn't hear another sound from Mac.

When all the tape was gone, they took the jar up to Scott's room and stuck it all the way in the back of his closet. They piled some old clothes in front of it. Then they shut the closet door behind them.

25

"**L**isten," Scott said to Glen three days later. He shook the cookie jar near Glen's ear.

Glen listened. "I don't hear a thing," he told Scott.

Scott shook the jar again, closer to Glen's ear. "Do you hear it now?" Scott asked.

Glen started to shake his head no. But he stopped himself. "Yeah," he answered. "It hardly sounds like anything at all."

"I think it worked," Scott said. "I think Mac's dried up into a little crystal again."

"I don't know," Glen replied nervously.

"It's been three whole days since he's been out

of water." Scott was trying to convince himself as much as Glen.

"Why can't we just throw this stupid cookie jar in the garbage and forget about it?"

"Because we've got to make sure that he's really gone," Scott told Glen. "And we'll never know for sure unless we look."

"I don't want to look!" Glen insisted.

"We've got to do it, Glen," Scott said, even though he didn't want to look either. "If we don't, we'll always be afraid Mac's going to come after us."

Scott took a deep breath and started peeling off the tape.

Glen jumped off the bed in a panic. "What if he *isn't* a crystal, huh? What if he's in there just trying to psych us out?"

"What do you mean?" Scott stopped peeling the tape.

"What if he's clinging to the sides of the stupid thing so we can't hear him moving around when we shake it?"

"There's nothing in there for him to cling to," Scott answered. And just to make sure he shook the jar again—as hard as he could.

Scott started peeling off the tape again. And

with every layer he unwrapped, he could see Glen turning whiter and whiter.

What if Glen was right? What if opening the jar was a big mistake?

Scott's hands were trembling as he pulled off the last piece of tape.

"If you open that up," Glen warned, "and he's in there—we're dead."

Scott knew that was true. But he had to do it. He had to know once and for all that Mac was out of their lives for good.

Scott held his breath. But as he pulled the lid off, the air that was trapped inside of his chest escaped in a huge sigh of relief.

"Glen!" Scott cried out excitedly. "It worked!"

"We did it!" Glen exclaimed. He high-fived Scott. "We got rid of Mac!"

For a minute the two boys sat on the bed, staring into the jar. Scott couldn't believe that it was finally over. He couldn't believe that the only thing left of the monster they had created was a tiny little black crystal.

"So what are we going to do with it?" Glen asked, finally breaking the silence.

"Nothing," Scott answered, as he reached for the lid of the jar. "We're never going to do anything with it ever again." Scott closed the cookie jar. "Until the day we die, Mac is staying a crystal. And he's staying right here."

Scott buried the jar in the back of his closet.

The battle was finally over.

The swimming, waving, disgusting little pig-monkey of a monster was definitely out of their lives for good.

26

"**D**on't even think about it!"

"Aw, come on, Glen," Scott begged. "Look how cool this is." Scott bit the inside of his lip so he wouldn't crack up in Glen's face.

Glen didn't even bother glancing at the ad Scott was waving in front of his nose. He just stared at Scott—as if he were insane.

"Wonder worms, Glen," Scott said, as he pointed to the ad in the comic book. "We've got to get them!"

"Are you out of your mind?"

Scott cracked up. He couldn't keep a straight face any longer. "Gotcha!"

"Not funny." Glen sighed. "Are we going to the mall or what?" he asked.

"Yeah. Yeah." Scott laughed as he threw the comic book down on his bed. "We're going. Just let me get my jacket."

Things are finally back to normal, Scott thought as he made his way to the closet. The video game place at the mall even had a new manager, so he and Glen could hang out there again.

Scott pulled open his closet door.

"Nooooo!" Scott screamed.

Nothing in his closet was where it had been when Scott took off for school that morning. All his clothes were hanging neatly. And all the shoes were lined up on the floor.

And the cookie jar was nowhere to be seen.

"What? *What?*" Glen yelled.

"My mother cleaned my closet!" Scott exclaimed. He didn't have to say another word for Glen to know exactly what the problem was.

"Mom!" Scott hollered, as he and Glen raced out of the room and down the stairs. "Mom!"

"I'm in the kitchen," she called back.

"Mom!" Scott ran into the kitchen with Glen right behind. "Mom," Scott repeated, trying to sound calm. "Did you by any chance clean my room today?" He already knew the answer.

His mother laughed. "So you noticed," she said over her shoulder as she bent down to get something out of the cabinet under the sink. "Maybe you can try to keep it that way for a while, huh?"

"Yeah." He told her what she wanted to hear, just so she would answer his next question. "When you were cleaning my room, did you find a cookie jar in my closet?"

"Yes," she answered, pouring detergent into the dishwasher. "As a matter of fact, I did. And do you mind telling me what my cookie jar was doing in the bottom of your closet?"

Scott ignored his mother's question and asked another one of his own. One that was much more important. "You didn't open it, did you?"

"Yes. I did." His mother stared at him as if he were nuts. She closed the dishwasher door. "But there was nothing in it."

"Are you sure?" Glen asked.

"I didn't see anything," she told him. "Just some crumbs. What are all these questions about?"

Scott ignored her again. "Well, what did you

do with it?" he asked. "What did you do with the cookie jar?"

"It's in the dishwasher," she answered, pushing the button to turn the dishwasher on.

"No!" Scott and Glen screamed. But it was already too late. They could already hear the sound of water spraying inside the machine.

"You two definitely need a hobby," Scott's mother said, as she turned and headed out of the room.

Scott and Glen stood frozen in horror.

They stared at the machine.

They stared as a giant monkey claw slammed out of the door of the dishwasher. Mac's giant monkey claw.

And he was definitely not waving.

GET READY FOR ANOTHER SPOOKY TALE
FROM FEAR STREET:

NIGHTMARE IN 3-D

R.L. STINE'S

GHOSTS OF
FEAR STREET ®

NIGHTMARE IN 3-D

NIGHTMARE IN 3-D

"You have to cross your eyes, Wes."

"No, you don't, Wes. You just have to cross one eye."

"That's wrong, you jerk. Just stare at the two dots until they look like three dots, Wes. Then look at the whole picture and you'll see it."

The "it" everybody was talking about was a stereogram—one of those pictures with a hidden 3-D image. Mr. Gosling showed us one in our sixth-grade science class today. We're studying optics and learning about how we see things.

It was lunchtime now, and my best friend,

Lauren, and two other kids in my class were trying to give me tips on how to see stereograms. But I knew they were wasting their time.

I mushed my gravy into my mashed potatoes and slid the carrots to one side of my plate. The carrots in the school cafeteria are always soggy.

"It's no use," I said, pushing my glasses up. "I just can't see 3-D."

"You can, Wes," Lauren insisted. "It just takes some practice. You'll get it."

That's what I like about Lauren. She thinks positive. Another thing I like about her is her bright blue eyes. They look so cool under her black bangs.

"What will Wes get?" Cornelia Phillips demanded, shoving in next to me at the table.

Cornelia is one of the horrible twins who live next door to my family. Her horrible sister, Gabriella, strutted up right behind her.

Gabriella slid her tray across the table, then sat down, too. As if we'd invited them or something.

"What will you get, Wes?" Gabriella repeated. They're both so nosy.

Then, while they waited for my answer, they both twirled their long blond ponytails. They wear

2

them coming out of the sides of their heads, only on different sides so you can tell them apart. Otherwise they're alike in every gross detail. They even snort alike when they laugh.

And I hear them snorting a lot because, as I said, the twins live next door to me—on Fear Street. Everyone has stories about the scary things that happen on Fear Street. But if you ask me, the twins are the scariest things on the block!

They're worse than the ghost that everyone says plays hide-and-seek with you in the woods—and tries to steal your body. Or that ghostly substitute teacher my friend Zack had.

I call the twins Corny and Gabby. Perfect names. Corny's always playing dumb practical jokes, mostly on me. She'll do anything to make me look like a total idiot.

And Gabby's always talking. She's the biggest gossip at Shadyside Middle School. And guess who most of her stories are about? That's right—me. Wes Parker.

"What will Wes get?" the twins demanded together, their voices growing higher and higher.

I tried to ignore them. That's what Lauren always tells me to do. I stared down at my plate and mashed my potatoes around some more.

3

When no one answered, Corny finally changed the subject.

"Did you ever see anything grosser than that cow eye Mr. Gosling dissected?" she asked. Then she wrinkled her nose and gazed at everyone. Waiting for an answer.

"We're eating lunch, Cornelia," Lauren reminded her.

"Yeah, I thought it was going to squirt right off the table when he cut it open," Gabby added, ignoring Lauren.

Lauren and I groaned and dropped our forks. The twins snorted together.

"Hi, Chad." Corny waved at Chad Miller at the next table. He's one of the cool kids. Chad didn't even glance at her.

"Hey, he smiled at you!" Gabby said. She twirled her hair with one hand and stuffed her face full of potatoes with the other.

Lauren rolled her eyes.

"Wow. This table is bor-ring!" Corny groaned.

"Yeah," Gabby agreed. She reached into her backpack and pulled out a poster. She spread it out on the table, practically pushing my tray off.

Oh, no, I thought. Another stereogram. The other kids leaned over to study it.

"Can you see it, Wes?" Corny asked in a fake sweet voice.

She knew I couldn't. I never can see them. But I stared at the poster and tried hard to see the hidden image.

No use.

"Uh-uh," I admitted. I felt really stupid. The twins can always do that to me. "I can't see it. I just can't see it."

Corny leaned across my tray. She was right in my face. "Well, then, you'd better eat your carrots."

Gabby rolled the poster up and both twins left, whispering to each other and snorting some more.

"They think they're a riot," I grumbled. "Eat my carrots. Very funny."

I gazed down at my carrots.

Gasped in disbelief.

And then let out a scream that shook the room.

2

My carrots stared back at me!

An enormous eyeball poked up from the middle of them.

I shoved my chair away from the table. It caught on a loose floor tile and flipped over backward—with me in it.

Then someone started to clap—slowly. I gazed up. It was Corny. She wore a big grin on her face.

Then Gabby joined in. With the same slow, loud clap.

Lauren helped me up. "You okay?" she asked.

I nodded and straightened my chair.

The whole cafeteria was clapping and laughing now. Even the cool kids.

I tried to smile as I sat back down.

I picked up my fork and forced myself to prod the cow eye. It rolled into the mashed potatoes.

"It's fake," I said to Lauren through clenched teeth. "It's only plastic." Then I began to stand.

"Where are you going?" she asked.

"I am going to get up—and kill the twins," I answered.

"Forget it," Lauren replied, tugging me back down. "It was just another one of the twins' stupid jokes. You have to ignore them."

I glanced around, searching the cafeteria for them, but they had vanished. "I'm not going to ignore them. Not this time," I said through clenched teeth. "This time I'm going to get even."

I still felt upset when school let out. Lauren and I decided to hang around in the Old Village before heading home.

"I don't care what you say, Lauren. This time I'm going to get back at the twins."

"What are you going to do?" she asked. "You're too cool to play any of their stupid jokes."

"I don't know . . ." I stopped short in the middle of the sidewalk. I felt as if someone had jerked me back by the hair. "Look!" I said, pointing into Sal's Five-and-Ten.

The twins' stereogram hung in the window. The one they showed us at lunch.

A sign over it read: MYSTERY STEREOGRAM— FIND THE HIDDEN IMAGE AND WIN A PRIZE!

"That's it!" I cried.

"What are you talking about?" Lauren asked.

"That poster is the same one the twins had at lunch," I explained. "So they must be trying to win the prize. If I can figure out the poster before they do, it will be the perfect revenge."

"All right! Let's go in!" Lauren cheered, leading the way into Sal's.

The ancient wooden floor creaked under our feet as we stepped inside. "It smells funny in here," I whispered. "Old and musty. And a little like rotting eggs."

"Whew," Lauren breathed. "It's really hot, too." She unzipped her jacket.

We wandered up and down rows of metal tables. Each was divided into sections by pieces of cardboard. None of the stuff seemed organized. Plastic

8

dolls sat next to piles of pot holders. Tubes of lipstick leaned against a stack of pocketknives.

And everything loose. Nothing came in boxes or wrapped in plastic.

"This store is really old and really weird," Lauren commented. She opened a lipstick to check the color. It was half used. Yuck.

We moved on.

Some old music played in the background. I recognized it. It sounded like the kind my grandfather plays when we visit him. Big band music, he calls it. It floated from a huge old radio.

I'd almost forgotten all about the Mystery Stereogram when a guy popped up from behind the back counter.

Lauren and I leaped back in surprise. He seemed to appear out of nowhere.

That must be Sal, I realized.

He dressed all in black and his hair was greased back. And he had an incredible mustache. It curled up and around to his cheeks. Really weird. But it wasn't the weirdest thing about him.

The weirdest thing was his eyes. They were enormous and watery, like the cow eye in class. And they bulged out from his eye sockets.

9

I took a step back and nearly knocked over a basket full of Mystery Stereograms. I lifted one out and unrolled it. "I . . . I want one of these," I said.

Sal blinked. "Oh. That," he snarled.

"Uh, I was wondering—how come there's a prize?"

"Is it a special kind of stereogram or something?" Lauren added.

Sal shook his head impatiently. "That has nothing to do with me." Then he turned his back to us.

I cleared my throat. "But it's in your window."

"Yes." He sighed, then spun around to face us again. "It *is* in my window. But I didn't put it there. The poster company did. They are offering the prize. I allowed them to hang it up. I thought it might bring in customers. No one wants to shop in five-and-tens anymore. Everyone is at the mall."

When he said "mall," he curled his lip and rolled his huge eyes. "I can't compete."

Lauren spread the poster out on the dusty glass counter.

I stared hard at its billions of tiny fluorescent dots. They were yellow, green, orange, and pink. But I couldn't see a picture inside it.

"I see only dots, Lauren," I admitted.

Lauren moved closer to the poster, then backed away. Then she smiled. "No big deal, Wes. Neither can I."

Sal reached out and grabbed the poster. "Good. Then that's settled." He started to shove it under the counter.

"But I want it," I protested. I had to get my revenge on the two monsters of Fear Street. "I have to figure out how to see it."

Sal frowned. "You can see it. You need only three things to see a stereogram."

I waited, holding my breath. Finally, someone was going to tell me the secret.

"You need a right eye. A left eye. And a brain." He smiled for the first time. He had big teeth, like a horse.

Some secret, I thought. Did he think I'd been trying to see stereograms without my brain? I handed my money over to Sal.

"You better be careful," he warned as he rang up the sale on his noisy old-fashioned cash register.

"Be careful of what?" Lauren asked.

Sal moved around the counter to stand close to me. He placed his face right up to mine and opened his eyelids wide. His big eyes bulged out more than ever now. I could see all these tiny red veins running through his eyeballs.

I tried to back away, but the basket of rolled-up posters stood directly behind me.

Sal stared at me so hard I felt as though he had X-ray vision. *"You* have the power to see more than most of us," he said in a creepy whisper.

I slid sideways to move away from him. This guy was beyond weird. "No, uh, I can't really see well at all. That's why I wear glasses."

"I am not talking about twenty-twenty eyesight. I am talking about true vision. *The power to see."*

He hissed the word *see* and his eyes bulged out even farther.

"Uh, it's getting kind of late," Lauren said. "We'd better get going, Wes." She smiled nervously.

I grabbed the poster from Sal. Then Lauren and I practically jogged down the aisle to the door. I gripped the door handle and pulled the door open—but a huge hand flew over my shoulder and slammed it shut.

I spun around.

Sal stared hard at me.

"Remember," he said again in that scary whisper. *"You* have the power to see. And some things are better left in two dimensions."

Lauren and I opened the door and hurried onto the sidewalk.

What did he mean by that? I wondered.

Why was he trying to scare me?

3

I was still trying to figure out what Sal meant when I reached home. *"You* have the power to see." Why did he keep saying that to me—and not to Lauren?

And why did he warn me to be careful?

I threw my jacket over one of the kitchen chairs and spread the Mystery Stereogram out on the table. I pinned it down with the salt and pepper shakers.

I stared and stared. "You have the power to see," Sal's words repeated in my head.

Ha! What did he know?

I couldn't see a thing.

I rubbed my eyes, wiped my glasses on my flannel shirt, and tried again.

I gazed at the poster close up.

I stepped back and stared at it from far away.

Close up again.

Then far away.

"What on earth are you doing?" Mom asked as she walked through the kitchen door, struggling with two huge bags of groceries. "Didn't you hear me honking the horn?"

"No. Sorry, Mom." Boy, I must have really been concentrating!

I went out to the car for the last two bags of groceries. As I entered the kitchen, Clawd, our cat, streaked between my legs and bolted through the kitchen and into the living room. He nearly sent me flying.

Outside I could hear a dog's annoying yipping. It was Fluffums, the twins' nasty little dog.

Fluffums attacks Clawd every chance he gets. He hates Clawd. It figures.

"Look what I bought," I said as Mom started unpacking the groceries. "It's a poster. I got it at the weird five-and-ten store in the Old Village."

Mom stopped and sniffed. "What's that horrible smell?"

I sniffed. "I think it's my poster. It smells like the store."

"Sal's Five-and-Ten?" she asked. "I haven't been in that strange little store in years."

"It's strange all right," I said. "Especially Sal." I sat down at the table. "Take a look at the poster."

Mom glanced at it.

"Cool, huh?" I asked.

"It really stinks," Mom said, covering her nose.

"Yeah, I know. But look at it, Mom. It's called a stereogram. And if you stare at it the right way, you can see a three-dimensional image hidden in it."

Mom folded a bag and leaned over the poster. "All I can see are a bunch of colored dots."

As Mom peered closer at it, my little sister, Vicky, ran into the kitchen. "Hey, Mom! Did you buy Froot Loops? Can I have a bowl now? Hey— is that 3-D?"

Vicky always does that. Asks a whole load of questions, one on top of the other. She doesn't even give you time to answer.

"Yes, no, and yes," Mom said. She's used to Vicky and her questions.

But Vicky wasn't even listening. She was staring at my poster. "Cool," she said, pushing her glasses up her nose. "There's one of these on the back of my cereal box. I'll show you." She reached up to the counter cabinet and pulled the box down.

We all studied it. It had lots of red and blue squiggles.

"It says there's a mouse hidden in the picture," Vicky said, "and I can see it. It's a big mouse."

I stared at the box. All I could see were the squiggles. "Hey, how do you do that?" I asked. I couldn't believe my little sister could see it and I couldn't.

Vicky shrugged. "I kind of cross one eye, like this." She peered up, and sure enough, behind her glasses I could see one eye gazing straight at me. The other was staring at her nose.

"Stop that, Vicky!" Mom exclaimed. "Your eyes will stay like that."

Vicky uncrossed her eye. "It says on the cereal box there are other ways to do it, too."

I read the directions off the back of the box.

"Press your nose against the picture. Then, very slowly, pull it away. Don't blink. As you look deeply into the picture, a 3-D image will appear!"

I tried it. No luck. Just a bunch of fat squiggles.

Mom tried it. "I feel silly." She laughed. She slowly pulled the cereal box away from her face. "No. Wait. I've got it! There is a mouse! He's eating something!"

I couldn't believe it. They had to be teasing me.

"Here. Try it again, Wes," Mom said to me. "It really works."

I held the box close, pressing it against my nose. The tiny red and blue designs were a blur. I pulled the box away slowly, my eyes wide open. Not blinking.

But I could feel my eyes struggling to refocus. And that's exactly what they did.

I was staring at squiggles.

No mouse.

No 3-D image.

I felt totally frustrated. "Okay," I said, holding the box up in front of them. "If both of you can see it so well, what's the mouse eating?"

Mom and Vicky peered at the picture together.

"Come on," I said. "What's it eating?"

"Swiss cheese," they sang out together.

I slammed the box on the table. "I'll do it," I silently promised myself. "Even if it kills me."

Clawd wandered back into the kitchen and jumped onto my lap. He tilted his head as he stared at the cereal box. Then he took a swipe at it, knocking the box over.

"I don't believe it!" I shouted. "Even the cat can see 3-D! Wait a second. If you're all so smart, tell me what's in this picture," I commanded.

I stood up and stabbed my finger at the Mystery Stereogram. Clawd jumped down and darted to a corner in the kitchen.

Mom and Vicky studied the poster. I could see Vicky crossing one eye again.

Mom shook her head. "No. I can't do that one."

Vicky's face was practically touching it. "Yuck!" she cried, backing away. "This thing smells like something rotten."

"Hah! You can't see it, either!"

"Let Clawd try," Vicky suggested. She carried it over to Clawd's corner, where he was licking a paw.

She held the poster up in front of him. He stopped licking his paw, but for a second he didn't put it down. He just kind of froze in place. And stared.

Then all his fur stood out. He looked as if he'd been in the clothes dryer or something. He arched his back and opened his mouth so wide that I could see every single one of his teeth. Even the ones all the way in the back.

Then he hissed and tore through the catflap faster than I'd ever seen him move.

Vicky shrugged. "Guess he didn't like it."

I rolled up the poster and said I was going upstairs to my room to do my homework. But instead of studying, I took my Shaquille O'Neal poster down from the wall by my bed and hung up the Mystery Stereogram in its place.

Now I could stare at it last thing at night, first thing in the morning.

I was determined to see 3-D. I was determined to win the contest.

I was going to beat those horrible twins.

"I'll start practicing this minute," I said aloud. "Homework will have to wait."

I sat cross-legged on my bed. First I'll try Vicky's way, I thought. The one-eye-crossed method.

But I quickly found out that I'm not very good at crossing one eye. I can cross two okay. But I could tell that crossing one at a time was going to take a lot of practice. And I didn't have that much time—if I was going to beat the twins.

Then I did what the cereal box said. I moved up real close to the poster. The tiny bright dots grew into a blur. Then I slowly inched backward on my bed.

I kept my eyes wide open.

I didn't blink.

My eyes started to burn. They were trying hard to focus.

I backed up a little more.

A little more.

Then—I fell out of bed.

"Wesley? What are you doing up there?" Dad was home from work.

"Just practicing my kung fu," I joked.

"Well, cut it out." Not a joke.

Clawd popped his head in the doorway.

"Come here, Clawd." I patted the bed.

The cat took a small step into the room. Then he noticed the poster. His ears flattened. His eyes narrowed. Then he turned and ran.

I flopped down on my bed and slipped off my glasses. I rubbed my eyes. They felt tired. I gazed

21

blankly at my wallpaper. The same wallpaper I've had since I was three years old. Rows and rows of toy soldiers.

Then I saw it! I couldn't believe it!

I rubbed my eyes and stared again.

Yes! One of the soldiers was moving. He was marching.

Marching off the wallpaper.

Marching toward me.

4

I bolted straight up in bed and jerked my head from the wallpaper.

I felt so dizzy. Did I really see what I thought I saw? Only one way to find out.

I slowly turned to face the wall and . . .

Nothing.

The toy soldier stood flat and still.

No marching.

No 3-D.

Same as always.

But I had seen a soldier move. I knew it.

I rubbed my eyes hard and concentrated—this time on the Mystery Stereogram. I felt my eyes relax.

Slowly all the tiny dots began to swirl. Orange, green, yellow, and pink dots flowed around the poster. Like lava spewing from a volcano.

I started to feel a little sick. The way I feel on a Ferris wheel. But I kept staring, not daring to blink.

I felt myself falling forward. As if something were trying to pull me into the poster. I grabbed a fistful of covers with each hand to anchor myself. But I didn't blink.

The dots spun around even faster. They seemed to surround me, trying to suck me in with the power of a huge vacuum cleaner.

Still—I didn't blink. And now the dots were forming a shape. A tree?

Yes! A tree!

And then I saw something in the tree. A bird? No, not a bird.

Something with a really long, skinny body. And two huge feelers.

And a big triangular head. And eyes! Two huge black eyes.

And finally I could see two long front legs

forming out of the dots. Two long legs with pincers on the ends!

A praying mantis!

That was it! I could see it! I could see in 3-D!

A praying mantis! Now I could claim the prize. I beat the twins!

I tried to blink, but my eyelids felt glued open. I couldn't break away.

I noticed even more details.

The mantis's jaws were large and powerful.

The eyes were wet and shiny.

It looked alive!

Something brushed against my neck. Then I felt tiny legs crawling over my cheek.

I dropped the covers and brushed the side of my face. My fingers touched something soft and fluttery. Ewww!

I swatted at it. I jerked my head back as it darted past my eyes.

A moth?

A sigh of relief escaped my lips. Get a grip, Wes, I told myself. This 3-D thing is making you jittery.

I watched the moth flutter around the room. And circle back. And hover in front of the poster.

Then something else caught my eye.

Nah. It couldn't be. No way.

I thought I saw the mantis twitch. I really *was* losing it.

I reached out and snatched the moth in midair. I held it in my fist. I could feel its wings beating against the palm of my hand.

Slowly I moved my fist to the left side of the poster.

Slowly I uncurled my fingers.

I could feel the moth crawl up my little finger. But I never tore my eyes from the mantis.

I watched it carefully.

I watched as it twisted its head to the left. I watched as it peered at the moth.

It peered at the moth!

The mantis really was alive!

Suddenly I heard Sal's words as clearly as if he stood in the room with me. "Some things are better left in two dimensions."

The moth flew from my hand and landed on the poster. Then it started crawling up the tree. Up to where the mantis lurked. Waiting.

I held my breath. My eyes began to water but I didn't dare blink. Not now.

The mantis's head moved slightly. Its feelers twitched. It held its front legs together. Just as if it were praying.

The moth climbed up the tree. Moved nearer and nearer to the mantis. Then one of the mantis's long front legs lashed out from the picture!

In one swift motion its huge pincers closed down on the moth and jerked it into the poster.

And I watched in horror as the mantis shoved the moth—wings and all—straight into its waiting mouth.

The mantis swallowed with a wet gulp.

Then its big eyes rolled hungrily toward me.

5

"**D**inner!" Mom shouted from downstairs.

I blinked.

"Wes, are you coming?" Dad hollered.

"Uh, yeah," I croaked.

My pulse raced. Something tickled my forehead. I jerked my hand up to swipe at it. Only tiny beads of perspiration dripping down my face.

I slid away from the poster and tried to stand up. My knees shook so badly I had to sit back down on the bed.

But I didn't look at the poster again. I wasn't ready.

I fumbled for my glasses and put them on with trembling hands. Calm down, I told myself. Just calm down.

When my breathing began to slow and my hands stopped shaking, I knew I had to take another peek at the poster.

Okay, here I go, I told myself firmly, trying to build up my confidence.

I slowly turned to face the poster, and my gaze was met with . . .

Colored dots.

Only colored dots.

No mantis.

And no moth.

I tried to think of a logical explanation. That's what Mr. Gosling, my science teacher, always tells us to do. But I couldn't come up with one. I decided I had to tell Mom and Dad. They were logical. Usually.

I joined my family at the dinner table. Mom had made spaghetti and garlic toast. My favorite. Too bad I wasn't hungry.

"Pass the Parmesan cheese, please," Dad said. He smiled. "Hey, I'm a poet and I don't even know it!"

"But your feet show it. They're Longfellows,"

Vicky finished for him. It was a silly game they always played.

"Uh, something strange just happened in my bedroom," I began.

"Mom, what's for dessert?" Vicky asked. "Can I have some more milk?"

"Frozen yogurt. Yes," Mom said, reaching for the milk.

"Is there any more spaghetti?" Dad asked.

They weren't paying attention to me. I had to make them listen.

"Here you go," Mom said, passing the bowl.

"I think my 3-D poster is coming alive!" I blurted out. That ought to get them.

Dad raised his eyebrows. "What do you mean, Wes?" he asked as he twirled his fork on his spoon, winding the spaghetti.

I cleared my throat. "I found a praying mantis in my poster, and it ate a moth that was flying around in my room."

"Yuck!" Vicky uttered, spitting out a mouthful of spaghetti. "That's disgusting!"

"So is that," Dad warned Vicky. He pushed his glasses up on his nose. "Wes, you probably just stared at it too hard. Your eyes can do funny things when they're tired."

"No, you don't understand," I protested. "I saw—"

Yeoow! Clawd raced through the catflap at full speed with a high-pitched screech.

Right behind him came Fluffums.

Our eyes followed the two crazed animals, but no one at the table moved. I don't think any of us could believe it. Fluffums. In our house.

Then someone pounded on the kitchen door. "Give us our dog back!" I heard one of the twins yell.

Hah! As if we'd invited the furry little rat in! For a second I didn't know whether to chase after the animals or go to the door and tell them off.

"I'll get the door," my father said.

"Wes, find Clawd," Mom ordered.

I searched the downstairs. Clawd wasn't there. So I dashed upstairs. Now I could hear Clawd yowling and Fluffums yipping. The sounds were coming from my bedroom.

When I hit the top step I froze. An agonizing yelp of pain echoed in my ears.

I tore down the hall, straight for my room. The first thing I spotted was Clawd, perched on my tall dresser. His back was arched and his fur stood straight out.

I gazed around the room for Fluffums. I couldn't find him.

Then I heard whimpering from the corner. The dog cowered there, his ears and tail down, his little body trembling.

Before I could make a move, the twins barreled in.

"Where's Fluffums?" Corny demanded. She shoved me out of the way. In my own room!

"Look! There! In the corner!" Gabby shouted. "I'll get him." She pushed past me, too, and reached down for the dog.

He growled. "I hope he bites her," I muttered under my breath.

"What's the matter, little Fluffums?" Gabby cooed in baby talk.

Fluffums whined and backed farther into the corner.

"Did that nasty old cat tease you again?" Corny added. She glared at Clawd—then at me.

I scooped Clawd up off the dresser. He clung to my shoulder. "Ouch!" I cried out as his claws sunk right through my shirt. He was in a real panic.

"Nasty cat." Gabby sneered, petting her dog. "He even claws his owner."

"Only when he's scared to death," I shot back.

32

"Come on, Baby Fluffy," Corny crooned. She swept the furball into her arms. She held him cradled in front of her like a baby.

"Oh, no!" Gabby shouted, pointing to the dog. "Look at his side! There's a patch of fur missing!"

"It was torn out!" Corny exclaimed. "By that horrible cat."

I stared at the dog's side. There *was* some fur missing. "Are you sure it wasn't missing before?" I asked. "Maybe he's going bald or something."

The twins went ballistic.

"He's not going bald, you jerk. Your stupid cat attacked him!" Corny shouted.

"We're going to tell our parents," Gabby threatened. "They've got a lawyer and he'll sue you. You and your cat and your whole family."

They stomped out of my room.

I stroked Clawd behind the ears. "You didn't do that—did you, Clawd?" I whispered. "You wouldn't hurt a fly."

Clawd started to squirm out of my arms. I let him go. He charged out of the room.

My eyes moved across the room to the poster.

What was that spot on the front?

I walked over and touched it.

Then a cold chill ran down my body.

6

The spot—it was white and soft.

Furry.

A clump of Fluffum's fur!

But that was impossible!

How did it get there?

Did the praying mantis . . .

No! Impossible!

I sprinted out of my room to tell Mom and Dad.

But on the way downstairs I overheard Mom say something so awful I had to stop and listen.

"I can't imagine how Clawd would cope." Mom sounded sad. "He's not a house cat. He loves to curl up in the backyard. Don't you think it would be cruel to lock him inside?"

Dad didn't answer right away.

What is he waiting for? He knows Clawd would hate being cooped up in the house.

"We have to think about it," he said finally. "This dog and cat situation has been the cause of a lot of problems."

I felt my face get hot. I'll straighten this out, I decided. All I have to do is tell them that Clawd didn't touch the twins' dumb little dog. All I have to do is tell them that it was the mantis.

Yeah, right. A 3-D mantis. Like they'll really believe me. Anyway, they'd probably think I was making the whole thing up to get Clawd out of trouble.

I turned around and crept back up the stairs to my room. My eyes darted to the mystery poster hanging over my bed. No way did I want to go to sleep anywhere near that, I thought.

My fingers shook as I reached over the bed toward the poster. What if one of those sharp green pincers shot out and grabbed me?

I tugged all four thumbtacks out as fast as I could. Then I grabbed the poster and rolled it up—tight.

35

Whew! Getting it off the wall felt good. I put my Shaq poster back up and felt even better. Maybe everything would turn back to normal now.

I decided to put the poster in my closet. I stuck it behind one of my failures—the hula hoop. The twins were hula hoop champions—of course. I could never get that thing to stay up.

But I didn't fail with the poster, I reminded myself. I could claim the prize from the poster company. I'd won it fair and square. For once, I'd beaten the twin monsters of Fear Street!

I rummaged around in my top desk drawer and found a postcard. "It's a mantis," I wrote on the card. Then I addressed it to the poster company. I printed my name and address in one corner and stuck a stamp on the other.

I decided to mail the postcard right away. I jumped down the stairs two at a time, told my parents I'd be right back, and jogged to the mailbox on the corner.

As I dropped the postcard in, I breathed a sigh of relief. I'd solved the Mystery Stereogram and mailed in the answer. I was finished with the poster. I felt great!

I glanced over at the twins' house as I walked

back home. I couldn't wait to see their faces when my prize arrived.

I imagined their reaction again and again as I climbed the stairs to my room. I could hear their angry little squeals. I could see their faces getting all red and scrunched up.

I sat down to do my homework, and before I knew it, it was time for bed. I was so tired! What a day!

I placed my glasses on the small table next to my bed. Then I punched my pillow a few times and turned off the bedside light. I wanted to dream about the moment the twins realized I'd beaten them.

But I couldn't fall asleep.

What was that strange light?

I sat up and glanced around.

I saw a faint glow. It came from under the closet door.

Did I leave the light on in my closet when I put the poster away?

I threw back the covers to hop out of bed. But I stopped when I saw the crack under the door begin to glow brighter and brighter.

With my eyes trained on the strange glow, I reached back, fumbled for the lamp switch—and sent the lamp crashing to the floor. The lightbulb shattered into a million razor-sharp pieces.

I quickly turned back to the closet door—and gasped!

A few bright fluorescent dots floated out from beneath it.

They shimmered like lightning bugs. Green, pink, orange, and yellow lightning bugs. They circled slowly, chasing one another.

Huh? Am I seeing things? I wondered. I knelt on the edge of my bed. Were my eyes playing tricks on me the way Dad thought? Had I fooled around with 3-D too much?

More dots floated out. More and more and more. Thousands of the dots streamed from under the closet door.

They bounced off the walls.

Careened off the furniture.

They swirled in lazy circles.

I gaped at them, frozen in horror. In disbelief. Swirling. Swirling.

And then, without warning, they started swirling around me!

And buzzing—an angry, grating buzz—the sound of a thousand hungry insects!

7

I pressed my hands against my ears as hard as I could, but I couldn't keep the noise out. I felt as if the buzzing dots were trapped inside my head. Crawling through my ears and behind my eyes.

The dots glowed brighter. They twirled around me faster and faster.

My eyes itched and burned. I wanted to rub them, but I was afraid to unblock my ears.

The itching spread through my entire body. Down my neck, my chest, around my back, over my arms and legs.

I squeezed into the corner of my bed. Then I quickly grabbed for my pillow and pulled it over my head.

I wanted to scream for help, but I was afraid to open my mouth. I was afraid the dots would fly inside me. Crawl down my throat and into my stomach.

A foul odor rose over my room. I could smell it through the pillow. Worse than a skunk or rotten eggs or spoiled milk.

My stomach lurched. My throat and nose burned. My entire body itched.

I had to do something!

I had to stop the swirling dots!

I released my grip on the pillow and grabbed my bedspread. I wound it around my arm. Then I dropped to my hands and knees and crawled toward the closet.

The buzzing grew almost unbearable without the pillow protecting my ears.

I forced myself to inch forward—until I reached the closet. The dots were still spilling out.

I shoved one edge of the blanket under the door. The dots kept coming. My fingers shook as I stuffed more of the blanket into the crack. I could feel the dots pushing against it. Struggling to get out.

I kept jamming the blanket under the door until it was wedged in tight. Then I backed up.

No light leaked from the closet.

I spun around.

All the dots in the room had disappeared.

I sat down carefully on the edge of my bed. I stared at the closet door. Waiting to see if the dots could escape my barricade.

I stared into the darkness for a long time. The room remained dark and silent.

The knots in my stomach disappeared. My hands fell open at my sides. I realized I'd been clenching my teeth, and I relaxed my jaws.

My breathing came slower and deeper. My eyes began drifting closed. I couldn't stay awake any longer. I crawled back under the covers and shut my eyes.

I flopped over onto my stomach—my favorite sleeping position. . . .

Crack!

The noise jerked me wide awake. It sounded like a tree being split by lightning.

Crack! There it was again.

The room was still dark, but I knew where the noise was coming from. The closet.

I crept slowly across the bed. My eyes locked on the closet door.

"No!" I cried as my eyes adjusted to the darkness. "This can't be!"

The door was bulging—bulging out into the room. The wood stretching and stretching—like a balloon about to pop.

Then I heard a *whooshing* sound. And the door seemed to suck itself back in.

Then it began to swell again. Pushing its way farther and farther into the room. The wood groaned and cracked. I could hear it splintering under the strain.

In and out.

In and out.

Every time the door swelled, the wood cracked some more.

The door was splitting open. Splitting right in two.

And then I spied it.

Jutting out through the split in the door.

A giant feeler.

8

"**H**elllp!" I screamed as I dived across my bed. I grabbed my glasses and shoved them on.

"Wes! Wes! What's wrong?" Mom stumbled into my room in her polka-dot nightgown and matching slippers.

She switched on the overhead light and sat down on my bed next to me. "Did you have a nightmare?" she asked, wrapping her arms around my shaking shoulders.

"No," I croaked. My tongue felt like cotton and I couldn't stop my teeth from chattering. "It's—

it's the m-m-mantis. He's trying to break out of the closet. He—"

Mom gave the closet a quick glance. "Slow down a minute, Wesley," she said, smoothing out my rumpled hair. "Take a deep breath and calm down."

I took a deep breath.

"Now, what did you say was in the closet?"

"The praying mantis. I tried to tell you at dinner," I said. "That's what was hidden in the Mystery Stereogram. You know, the one I got from Sal's Five-and-Ten?"

Mom gave a hesitant nod.

"Well, it's alive. And it can get out of the poster."

Mom rolled her eyes.

"You've got to believe me," I pleaded. "The mantis ate a moth that landed on the poster. And Fluffums."

"It ate Fluffums?" Mom exclaimed.

"No, no. The mantis pulled that clump of fur out of him. That's why I put the poster away in my closet. It's dangerous. It's really dangerous. And now the mantis almost smashed through the closet door."

Mom stared hard at the closet door again, then

44

peered around my room. My lamp lay on the floor with the shade knocked off. Pieces of the broken lightbulb were scattered everywhere. And my bedspread was stuffed under the closet door.

"I think we should open the closet and look inside, Wes," Mom said, patting my shoulder.

"I d-don't think that's a good idea, Mom," I stammered.

"Now, come on, Wes," she crooned. "We'll open up the closet door, and you'll see—everything will be fine. Just fine."

I forced myself over to the closet, tiptoeing around the pieces of broken glass. I examined the door closely. It seemed okay.

I rubbed my hand over the wood.

Smooth. No cracks. Not even a splinter.

Mom padded up beside me. "Now," she said patiently, "open the door."

I hesitated for a second. Yes, I decided. Mom was right. I had to open the closet. I had to know if the mantis was still waiting for me.

I slowly pulled the bedspread out from under the door.

My eyes were glued to the crack at the bottom.

No light. No dots. No buzzing sound. Safe so far.

Mom reached over my shoulder and turned the doorknob. A cold chill ran down my spine. Huge drops of perspiration dripped from my forehead. My pajamas began to stick to me.

"Hmmm. It seems to be stuck," Mom said. She twisted the doorknob both ways and pulled harder.

"No! Don't!" I shouted. I grabbed her wrist.

"Your hands are like ice cubes!" she exclaimed.

"I'm scared!" I admitted, gripping her arm tighter. "Maybe the mantis doesn't want us to get in. Maybe it's holding the door shut."

Mom gave me a quick hug. "It's okay," she said softly. "These old wooden doors just get sticky sometimes."

She tried the doorknob again. This time it turned.

My temples pounded. My pulse began to race. I held my breath as she slowly opened the door.

But I didn't look inside. I couldn't. I just studied her face. Waited for her reaction. But her expression didn't change.

She reached into the closet. Pulled on the chain that switches on the closet light. "Seems to be okay," she said. Then she stepped back so I could see inside.

My heart hammered in my chest as I pushed up my glasses to peer into the closet.

Everything seemed—normal.

Just as I'd left it.

The poster still lay behind the hula hoop—still tightly rolled up.

I shoved a couple of shirts aside. Nothing behind them.

I studied the lightbulb in the closet ceiling. Normal.

I felt the inside of the door. No cracks.

A sigh escaped my lips.

I shuffled over to my bed and collapsed into it. My arms and legs had turned to limp noodles. "Maybe it *was* a nightmare," I mumbled.

"They can feel awfully real," Mom answered. She picked up my lamp and returned it to the nightstand. "I'll be right back. I want to sweep up that broken glass before you cut your feet."

As soon as Mom left, I bolted over to the closet door and stuffed the bedspread back into the crack. This wasn't a dream. This was real. And I wasn't taking any chances.

When I heard Mom's slippers clomping back toward my room, I leaped back in bed. She handed me a new lightbulb, and I screwed it into my lamp right away. She didn't ask me about the bedspread—even though I know she noticed it shoved back under the door.

Mom swept the bulb pieces into a dustpan and emptied them into my wastebasket. "Should I switch this off, Wes?" She pointed to the overhead light.

"That's okay, Mom. I'll get it."

"Good night, Wes," she said. "Call me if you need me."

"Good night."

"Good night. What a joke, I thought. This was the worst night of my life. And it wasn't over yet.

I felt okay with Mom in the room. But as soon as she left, I couldn't stop staring at the closet. Waiting for something to happen. Something bad.

I thought maybe I should take the poster out to the garbage. But then I imagined the mantis escaping from the poster, bursting through the front door, and crawling up here to strangle me in my sleep.

No. Taking it outside wouldn't help.

I decided to bring the poster to school tomorrow and show it to Mr. Gosling. He's a scientist. Kind of. Maybe he'd have a logical explanation.

I left on all the lights. I propped the pillows

against the headboard so I could watch the closet. And just to be extra safe, I left my glasses on. Now I'd be ready to run if the dots came back.

Would they come floating out again?

Would they?

I vowed to stay up all night to find out.

9

Bzzzz. Bzzzz. Bzzzzz.

The dots are back!

I leaped out of bed and charged out of my room. I stood in the empty hallway, trying to catch my breath. My chest heaved up and down. I started to wheeze.

Bzzzzz. Bzzzzz. Bzzzzz.

Wait a minute. I knew that sound.

I stood up against the doorframe and peeked into my room.

No dots.

My alarm clock—ringing. Only my alarm.

I hurried back into my room and shut off the clock. Then I checked out my room.

The lights were still on.

My bedspread was still stuffed under the closet door.

I had made it through the night. Somehow.

I felt so relieved—until I realized I couldn't get dressed without opening the closet to get my clothes.

I crept over to the closet door and pressed my ear against it. No sounds. No insects buzzing.

I knelt and slid the bedspread out from under the crack. Then I opened the closet with a quick jerk.

No mantis!

I grabbed a pair of jeans and my red flannel shirt and pulled them on. I stuffed my feet into my socks and high-tops. Then I lifted the poster with two fingers. The paper felt damp and sort of sticky. I slid it into my backpack and raced downstairs.

I couldn't wait to talk to Mr. Gosling. He knew all about optics. He had a scientist's mind. He'd help me figure this out.

"You okay this morning?" Dad asked. He began slicing a banana over his cornflakes.

"Uh—sure," I answered. I shook some cereal into a bowl and splashed on some milk. "Just a bad dream," I added. I didn't want to talk to my parents about the mantis again until I figured out what was going on.

I wolfed down the cereal and chugged a glass of apple juice. "Got to go," I called. I slipped my backpack on and headed for the door.

Clawd wound himself around my legs. I bent over to pet him, and the poster started to slide out of my backpack. "Yeooww!" Clawd tore away from me like a streak of lightning.

I sighed. "Bye," I called again and left. I had to get some answers today.

As I walked to school, I kept reaching back and touching the poster. Making sure it was still there. I felt as if I had some sort of monster trapped in a bottle. And I didn't want it to get loose.

I felt extra glad when I spotted Lauren waiting for me at our usual corner. She was wearing a bright blue jacket that matched her eyes. And she had her black hair pulled back with a matching headband.

Lauren frowned as I jogged up to her. "Hey, Wes, you look wrecked. Are you okay?"

"Not really," I admitted. I reached back and touched the poster again.

We turned onto Hawthorne Street, and I told Lauren about everything. The mantis. The moth. Clawd, Fluffums, the real, live nightmare in my bedroom last night. And my plan to ask Mr. Gosling for help. I talked nonstop.

When I finally finished, we were a block away from school. "Well, what do you think?"

"Uh," Lauren started. She chewed her lip for a minute. "Wes, this isn't a joke or anything, is it?" she asked. "I mean, is this a story you're just trying out on me? Before you tell it to the twins?"

"Of course not!" I protested. "I wouldn't joke about something like this. It's too weird. Besides, why would I try to fool you?"

"Okay, okay." Lauren held her hand up. "But you have to admit—it is a really strange story."

"I know. But you *do* believe me, don't you?"

"Sure," Lauren said. But I could tell she really wasn't sure. "Talking to Mr. Gosling is a good idea," Lauren continued. "He's logical and all. Maybe he can figure it out. Anyway, whatever happens, Wes, remember—you beat the twins!"

"Yeah. I did. I almost forgot." We laughed and slapped each other a high five.

Then Lauren's face turned serious. "You know—maybe that creepy guy in the five-and-ten was right. Remember, he kept saying, 'You have the power to see.' Maybe it has something to do with that."

Lauren was really starting to believe me!

We crossed the street. A lot of kids were already hanging around outside the school.

"Hey, there's Kim." Lauren pointed to a red-haired girl wearing bright green leggings and a matching jacket. "I have to borrow her history notes. See you later," she called as she ran ahead. "And be careful!"

"See you later," I called, turning up the cobblestone walkway alone.

I reached back one more time to touch the poster—and something yanked me hard from behind. I stumbled backward.

I tried to turn. But it held both my arms in a tight grip.

I tried to scream. But no words came out.

I struggled to escape, but the more I twisted, the tighter it clung to me. Tighter, tighter. Hauling me right off the sidewalk.

I felt something sharp dig into my neck. Something sharp—like pincers.

10

"**H**elp!" The word exploded from my throat. "Somebody help me!" I twisted and fought to get free.

And then the thing released me.

I thudded to the ground—and spun around.

The "thing" had four arms. And four legs. And tails growing out of the sides of two ugly snorting heads.

Corny and Gabby.

I sighed and pushed myself to my feet. I felt like a total jerk.

They stared at me, giggling and snorting. "Got you, huh?" Corny taunted.

"Yeah," I shot out. "You're a riot. A real riot. Corny."

"Don't call me that!" Corny scowled.

"Yeah, don't call her that," Gabby echoed, twirling her ponytail.

"Your family owes our family money," Corny announced. "Money for the vet bills our parents had to pay." She narrowed her eyes.

"Lots of money." Gabby sneered.

"And that's not all," Corny jumped in. "The police are going to take your vicious cat away, too."

I could feel my face grow red-hot. I wanted to lunge for the twins and yank them around by their stupid ponytails. "No way! *Your* dog ran into *our* house," I insisted.

At least I beat them at the contest, I thought. And the second my prize arrives, I will rub it in their faces. I will never let them live it down.

But for now I would have to follow Lauren's advice—and ignore them.

Without another word I adjusted my backpack, turned, and left.

* * *

I met Lauren at the lockers right before science. I'd gotten through the first couple of hours of school with no problems. I told her what the twins said that morning about the police taking Clawd away.

"They're making it up. They're such jerks," she said, slamming her locker shut with an extra-loud bang.

I shoved my math book into my locker and hung my jacket on the hook. Then, very carefully, I inched the poster out of my backpack. "I'm going to try and catch Mr. Gosling before class starts."

"Good idea," Lauren agreed.

I turned to go—and a hand reached out from nowhere and snatched my glasses off.

I spun around and dropped the poster. It unrolled on the floor.

"Hey! I can't see!" I yelled. "Give me my glasses back!"

The twins! Those jerks! They had my glasses. They always steal my glasses. They know I can't see without them.

I can't wait to teach those twins a lesson, I fumed.

I heard the twins snorting and giggling all the way up the stairs. They were in Mr. Gosling's class, too. I'd get my glasses back then. But first, I had to find Mr. Gosling.

"Come on, Wes," Lauren interrupted my thoughts. "The bell's about to ring."

I squatted down next to the poster. I wanted to roll it up right away. It felt safer that way.

I tried not to peer directly at the poster. It still scared me—a lot. Instead, I glanced at the tile floor next to the poster. But my eyes were drawn to the colored dots as I rolled it up.

I glanced at it for only a second. But that's all it took.

There it stood.

The mantis.

Staring back at me—with its huge, wet, shiny eyes.

I jumped back in horror and screamed, "It's back! It's back!" I couldn't stop screaming. "It's back!"

"Wes! Wes! What's wrong?" Lauren cried.

I couldn't answer. I could only stare. Stare at the mantis as it fought its way out of the poster.

It twisted and strained, like a prehistoric monster trapped in a tar pit. And all the time it watched me. Watched me with those terrifying bug eyes.

Do something. Do something! a voice cried out inside me. But my feet froze to the floor.

I heard Lauren yelling. But she sounded so far away. I was in some kind of trance. The blood pounded in my temples. My heart felt about to burst out of my chest.

DO SOMETHING! the voice screamed in my head.

I grabbed the poster.

My fingers fumbled as I began to roll it up.

I could feel the mantis pushing, pushing against my curled fingers.

I kept rolling up the poster. Faster. Faster.

And then I lost my grip—and the poster sprang open.

"Ahhh!" I yelled as two long back feelers lunged out and dug into my hands.

I dropped the poster.

The feelers waved wildly in the air as it fell. I slammed my foot down to smash them—and missed. The mantis buzzed furiously.

I stomped again. Harder.

One of its long, spindly legs rose out of the poster. And its razor-sharp pincer locked around my ankle.

"Ow!" I howled, shaking my leg wildly. "It's got me! It's got me!"

"What's happening?" Lauren cried. "What's got you?"

She couldn't see it! The mantis had exploded right out of the poster. It was huge! And she still couldn't see it.

It quivered and shook as it freed itself from the paper.

And it began to grow larger. Much larger than the size of the poster!

"Lauren," I gasped. "It's the mantis. It's out of the poster! It's attacking me! And it's huge!"

The mantis reared up on its back legs. It shot out a pincer and gripped my wrist. And squeezed. Squeezed until my hand felt numb. Squeezed until my fingers turned purple.

I clawed at the pincer, trying to tear it off me.

The mantis's legs lashed out. The sharp barbs tore at my shirt. Ripped right through it. My body stung and burned as its pincers pierced my skin.

It continued to grow. Up. Up.

Now it stood as tall as me!

Its enormous, ugly bug face stared into my eyes. Then its feelers shot through my hair.

"Get it off me!" I screamed again and again.

My arms and legs flailed madly as I tried to struggle free. The mantis wrapped its strong, spindly arms around my neck.

Was it trying to choke me?

Where was Lauren? Why wasn't she helping? "Laur—" Her name stuck in my throat as I gasped for air.

I jerked my head up to try to loosen the huge insect's deadly grip.

"Lauren? Where are you?" I choked out.

"Lauren? Lauren?"

"Lauren?"

I saw her. Hurrying down the hall.

Leaving me to fight the giant mantis!

"Aaaagggghhh." A gurgling sound escaped my throat as the mantis squeezed tighter. I couldn't breathe. Bursts of color exploded before my eyes.

I flung my head back.

I stumbled through the hall with the mantis clutching my throat.

Then I whirled around and slammed the mantis into the row of lockers. I heard that high-pitched buzz again, and I felt the pincers loosen.

The insect opened its huge jaws. I could see deep into its mouth. I could smell its sour breath. It snapped its jaws shut inches from my face.

I shoved one arm between the creature and my chest and hurled it from my body. It crashed to the floor with a horrible screech.

Then I spotted Lauren. Leaning against the lockers with her arms folded.

"Very convincing, Wes." She smiled. "If I didn't know better, I'd swear you were wrestling with a huge, invisible praying mantis."

She reached out her hand and gave me a playful shove. "We're going to be really late if—"

The mantis lashed out and locked a pincer around Lauren's wrist.

"Owww! Wes!" she screamed. "Something's got me! Get it off!"

I took a deep breath and gave a sort of karate chop to the mantis's long front leg.

The mantis cried out and flew across the hallway.

"W-what happened?" Lauren stammered, rubbing the red, raw spot where the mantis had sunk its pincer.

"The mantis," I whispered. I watched as its big head slowly turned and its enormous eyes scanned the empty hall. "It's still here, but it's not looking at us right now. Wait. I think it sees something down the hall."

I squinted, but I couldn't see very well—things were a total blur without my glasses.

"It's Mr. Gosling!" Lauren cried. "Quick, Wes! Stop him and tell him about the mantis."

Lauren couldn't see the mantis. But at least she really truly believed me now.

Mr. Gosling ambled down the hall balancing a high pile of books under his chin.

He headed straight for us.

And the mantis.

"Look out!" I yelled.

Too late.

The mantis seized his ankle and sank its jaw into it.

Mr. Gosling let out a low moan. His long legs buckled underneath him. He tumbled face-first on the floor and slid down the hall on his stomach. Dragging the mantis behind him.

I snatched up one of the books he dropped— *Fun with Insects.* I stuck it in my back pocket. It might come in handy, I thought.

I grabbed another book and hurled it at the mantis.

Missed!

"Wes, what are you doing?" Lauren whispered.

"Trying to hit the mantis," I said.

I heaved another book at it.

"Darn! Missed again."

"Where is it, Wes?" Lauren asked. "What's it doing?"

I squinted down the hall. Mr. Gosling climbed to his feet. "It had Mr. Gosling by the ankle," I answered. "Now it's lying right behind him."

"I'd like an explanation," Mr. Gosling bellowed as he strode toward us. His baggy gray cardigan flapped behind him. "Why are you throwing those books? And who tripped me?"

I knew this wasn't the time to get Mr. Gosling's theories about the poster. I had to talk fast. "Uh. No one tripped you. At least Lauren and I didn't trip you. But I did throw your books. I'm sorry about that. But I had to—"

"Had to throw books?" Mr. Gosling questioned me, staring over his glasses. "We'll deal with this later. Now, please help me pick them up." He bent over and started gathering his books.

Lauren and I helped. I kept one eye on the mantis the whole time.

"Quick, Lauren," I whispered. "It's coming!"

"Run for it!" she screamed, dropping her pile of books and sprinting down the hall.

Mr. Gosling pushed himself to his feet and patted his tie down. "What is wrong with her? She threw my books on the floor. I really don't understand this behavior. Maybe you'd both better come with me for a serious talk."

"No, please, Mr. Gosling," I begged. "There's a logical explanation for all this. I'm sure there is. But I need you to help me figure it out."

"Figure it out?" Mr. Gosling asked. "You want me to figure out why *you* are misbehaving?"

"Where is it? Is it gone?" Lauren yelled from halfway down the hall, her voice high and squeaky.

"No," I called.

I studied the mantis, trying to decide what it would do next. It had stopped crawling. Now it seemed to be waiting. Almost motionless. Then, very slowly, it rubbed one of its pincers on the top of its head.

Then it took a step toward Mr. Gosling.

"It's getting closer," I warned.

"What's getting closer?" Mr. Gosling demanded.

I swallowed hard.

67

"Tell him!" Lauren urged. "Tell him before it's too late!"

"Too late for what?" he asked. "Class?" He sounded more confused than angry now.

"Um. Yes. Class," I answered. "Let's go." I scooped up the books Lauren had dropped. I grabbed Mr. Gosling's elbow and quickly steered him around the mantis and over to the stairs.

Lauren started to climb up first.

"Wait!" I yelled. "Where's the poster? I have to have the poster!"

"There!" Lauren pointed. "Near the lockers."

I ran down the hall and scooped it off the floor. As I rolled it up, I noticed a large blank space. The space where the mantis had been.

Lauren raced down the hall, tugging my arm. "Come on," she urged, searching the hall for some sign of the creature. "Where is the thing?"

"It's okay," I answered. "It's busy."

Mr. Gosling stood by the staircase rearranging the books in his arms. The mantis crouched nearby. But it wasn't paying any attention to him. It held its two front legs together in front of its huge eyes.

"Busy doing what?" Lauren asked. I could tell she was working to stay calm.

68

"It's behind Mr. Gosling. Don't worry, it doesn't seem interested in him. It looks as if it's praying or something," I whispered.

Lauren wrenched my arm. "Doesn't that mean it's getting ready to attack?"

12

Yes!

Lauren was right!

Now I remembered. The mantis had raised its legs in a praying position right before it ate the moth!

"Let's get out of here!" I shouted.

The mantis began rocking back and forth, with its front legs pressed together.

We raced over to Mr. Gosling. I grabbed for his sleeve, yanking him up the steps.

"Be careful, Wes," he warned. "I'm going to

drop these books again. It doesn't matter if we're a few minutes late."

"Don't want to be any later than we already are," I replied.

"That's right," Lauren agreed.

I heard that terrible buzzing sound—like a million angry mosquitoes. Lauren didn't seem to hear it at all. I glanced over my shoulder.

"It's still behind us," I whispered to Lauren as we reached the top of the stairs. "It's crawling up. Following us!"

"Tell him!" she urged.

We had almost reached the science lab. I jumped in front of the door, blocking it. "Mr. Gosling, there's something you have to know. It's about the stereogram. The one the twins brought to class. There's a mantis in it. A praying mantis. And it's not just 3-D. It's actually alive—"

Mr. Gosling pushed past me. "After class," he answered. I could tell he was fed up.

Lauren and I hurried to our seats. She sits in the back of the class. I sit near the front, right next to the twins.

"Give me back my glasses," I ordered them.

"What glasses?" Corny asked.

"Yeah, what glasses?" Gabby chimed in.

"My glasses, you—"

I heard a horrible scraping sound at the door. It opened a crack and two long black feelers poked inside. They waved back and forth—searching the air. Searching for something.

"Oh, no!" I moaned.

I turned to Lauren. "It's here!" I mouthed.

"Is there something you would like to share with the rest of the class, Wes?" Mr. Gosling asked.

"Umm, I really need to talk to you about the 3-D poster." I glanced at the door. It swung open wider. The mantis's huge head appeared. Its jaws dripped saliva. "Someone might get hurt if—"

"I told you—we will talk about the poster after class," Mr. Gosling said sternly. Then he began to make his way over to the door.

I wanted to cover my eyes with my hands. Or disappear under my desk. But I knew I had to warn Mr. Gosling. I jumped up from my seat—but I wasn't fast enough.

Mr. Gosling reached the door and—shut it hard, smashing one of the mantis's back legs.

Phew. That was a close one.

The mantis's leg re-formed itself. The buzzing

72

grew louder than ever. I could feel it vibrating through my body. My ears pounded. I covered them with my hands, trying to block out the hideous noise.

"But after class will be too late—" I tried to warn Mr. Gosling.

"After class!" Mr. Gosling exclaimed. "And please don't cover your ears when I'm speaking to you."

The twins started to snort.

I thought my eardrums were going to explode.

"Yes!" I shouted. "I hear you."

"Why are you shouting? What's wrong with you today, Wes?" Mr. Gosling asked. "Are you sick?"

"No," I muttered. I wished I could tell him yes. Then he would send me down to the nurse. The nurse would call my mom. And my mom would come and take me home.

But it was too late for that.

I bought the poster.

I ignored Sal's warnings.

And now I was the only one who could see the mantis. I was the only one who could hear the buzzing. So I had to stay. I had to stop the mantis. If I could.

73

"Let's continue our study of the eye," Mr. Gosling started.

The buzzing slowly faded, but the mantis remained perched by the door. Mr. Gosling began pacing back and forth in front of the classroom—the way he always does. His hands shoved deep into his pockets.

The mantis crept up behind him and followed him—back and forth across the room. Back and forth. It paused when Mr. Gosling paused. It turned when Mr. Gosling turned.

I wanted to scream.

At least it's not praying, I thought. But the mantis definitely had its eye on Mr. Gosling.

Mr. Gosling turned to the chalkboard and drew a side view of the human eye. The mantis reached out to take a swipe at him.

It missed.

I let out a loud gasp.

Mr. Gosling glared at me. Then he turned back to his drawing.

The mantis tried again.

This time its pincer hit the chalkboard.

Screeeech.

Everybody cried out. A few kids held their

hands over their ears. Mr. Gosling glared at me again. As if it were my fault!

At first I was surprised that everyone could hear the *screech*. Then I remembered that other people couldn't see the mantis or hear it buzzing—but they could feel it grab them. So I guess it made sense that they could hear its pincer scraping the chalkboard.

Mr. Gosling slammed the chalk in the rack and marched over to a corner of the room—where his favorite specimen stood under a white sheet.

"Okay," he announced, whipping the sheet off. A human skeleton hung from a stand. It was a little shorter than Mr. Gosling. "We're going to examine the skull today."

The mantis inched over to the skeleton. Its feelers were waving all over the place. It tilted its enormous head, staring hard at the bones. Saliva dripped from it jaws and puddled at its feet. It was hungry, I realized.

I was so nervous, I fumbled with my ruler and it crashed to the floor.

Mr. Gosling ignored me. He rolled the skeleton closer to the class. "Have a look at the bones around your eyes."

"Ooh, gross!" Gabby cried.

Everybody laughed.

The mantis leaned forward and seemed to be sniffing the skeleton. I leaned forward, too. My stomach heaved.

The mantis caught the skeleton's hand between its gaping jaws. It started chewing the finger bones.

The whole class gasped. "Cool trick!" someone yelled.

"I think it's hungry," I mouthed to Lauren.

Mr. Gosling stared at the arm. It looked as if it were waving to us.

"Who's doing that?" Mr. Gosling demanded. "Wes?"

"No!" I protested. "But you have to listen to me. I think it's *really* dangerous now. I think it's hungry."

"What's hungry?" Gabby asked. "The skeleton?"

A few kids laughed.

"It sure looks thin," Corny added.

More laughter.

The mantis grabbed one of the skeleton's legs and started gnawing on the knee.

"What's it doing now?" Gabby called.

"I think it's the cancan," Corny cracked.

The class went completely out of control. They thought the whole thing was a big joke.

Mr. Gosling grabbed the stand and wheeled the skeleton away from the mantis. "This is not a toy," he declared. "I want an apology from the person responsible."

The room fell silent. Except for the sounds coming from the mantis—buzzing and snapping its pincers recklessly in the air. "Don't move the skeleton!" I cried. "You're making it angry!"

The class exploded into laughter.

Mr. Gosling strode over to my desk. He glared down at me. "If I hear one more outburst, you are out of here. Do you understand that?" he growled. "And I don't mean detention. I mean suspension. From school!"

What could I say?

I felt so helpless. I needed to explain everything to Mr. Gosling. To get him on my side.

I placed my head in my hands. Think, Wes. Think.

Then I jerked my head up. Where was the mantis? I'd lost track of him.

77

Oh, no! I slid down in my seat.

The creature had discovered the corner in the back of the room where we kept the class animals.

I thought of the moth.

I remembered Fluffums and the clump of hair.

And I watched in horror as the creature reached its pincer out to the hamster cage.

13

I stared in horror as it pulled the bars of the hamster cage apart.

I closed my eyes for a moment. Trying to come up with a plan. But a terrifying picture crowded my mind. I saw the mantis shove the hamster into its waiting, dripping jaws—and swallowing it whole. I imagined it moving on to the guinea pigs, the white mice, and the baby frogs.

Here goes, I thought. I'll probably be expelled from school—but I had to take action.

I climbed up on my lab stool. "Free the animals!" I shouted to Lauren. At least that way maybe they wouldn't be sitting targets. Maybe they could run and hide.

Lauren jumped up and ran to the frog aquarium. She scooped up the frogs, two and three at a time, and plunked them on the floor.

They sat there frozen.

The mantis plodded toward them.

They slowly lifted their little heads in the air. They seemed to be sniffing. Then they started hopping in all directions.

Some of the kids began to scream and climb on top of their desks. Most of the kids were laughing.

"Stop that this instant!" I could barely make out Mr. Gosling's voice above the noise.

Lauren ignored him and moved on to the next cage.

"Free them all!" I shouted. I ran to the chalkboard and grabbed the wooden pointer.

"What do you think you're doing?" Mr. Gosling demanded. He grabbed my shoulder and shook it hard.

"Look out!" I yelled as I broke free from his grasp. I charged over to the animal cages, waving the pointer like a sword.

The mantis stood over a cage full of fat white mice. Drooling and praying.

Rocking back and forth.

The mice squeaked wildly, jumping up and down like pieces of popping popcorn.

I made my way carefully to the mantis. The pointer kept slipping from my sweaty palm. I crept up behind the creature and jabbed its side. It spun around and yanked the stick right out of my hand—but it backed off a few feet, buzzing furiously.

I knocked the mice cage over and urged the mice out.

"What are you doing with those mice?" Mr. Gosling exclaimed, throwing his hands up in the air.

"I'm saving their lives!" I answered, clapping loudly so they would scatter.

"What about the turtles?" Jimmy Peterson called out. Everyone was getting into it now.

"Let them go, too!" I commanded. And he did.

The turtles wouldn't move—no matter how much anyone yelled at them. A few kids picked them up so they wouldn't get squashed.

Someone let the garter snake go. The mantis lunged for it. But the snake wriggled under the radiator in a flash. The mantis sent a pincer out, but it couldn't reach.

"Good!" I shouted. Now I turned to the bat's cage.

"Not my bat!" Mr. Gosling pleaded, clutching his chest.

The bat was Mr. Gosling's favorite class pet. He found it on a hiking trip. Its wing was broken and Mr. Gosling nursed it back to health. Mr. Gosling would want me to set the bat free if he could see the mantis, I convinced myself.

I flung the black cover off the cage and pulled open the door. The mantis lumbered in our direction. The bat didn't move. It hung from its branch, all wrapped up in its wings.

"It's asleep!" I yelled to Lauren. "And the mantis is headed right for it!"

"Tickle it!" she called.

I brushed it lightly on its underside with my finger. That did it. The bat woke up and burst through the door, excited to be free.

"Get him! Get him!" Mr. Gosling yelled, chasing after the bat.

Someone opened the door to let the mice out, and the bat escaped into the hallway.

Mr. Gosling ran out the door and slammed it behind him.

Suddenly the classroom went quiet. The kids

stopped shouting. All the animals had found hiding places.

It felt creepy.

"Where is it now?" Lauren whispered.

"It's n-not near us," I stammered. "It's poking around Corny's desk."

"Hey! Who knocked my microscope over?" Corny whined. She hurried back to her desk. Gabby was right behind her. But the mantis was no longer there. It had moved on.

What would it do next? I wondered.

"Ooh, my notes are all wet," Gabby complained. "And slimy." She picked them up by the corner.

"Mantis drool," I whispered to Lauren.

"Where is it now?" she asked.

"It's—it's coming this way."

I spotted the pointer on the floor. I snatched it up and crouched under one of the lab tables. My knees trembled and my hands shook.

"What are you going to do?" Lauren asked. She crouched beside me.

"I'm—I'm going to try to stab it with the pointer," I said, inching toward the mantis. I could see its thin green legs as it wobbled down one row and up another.

My pulse started to race as it crawled closer and

closer. A few more feet—and I'd be able to reach it.

Then the bell rang.

"Lunch!" someone shouted.

The kids gathered up their stuff and stampeded out the door. The mantis joined the crowd.

"Where is it now?" Lauren demanded.

"It's—it's gone," I answered.

"Great!" Lauren cheered.

"There's just one problem." I sighed.

"What?" Lauren asked.

"It's headed for the cafeteria."

"**D**on't go!" Lauren shouted as I ran out the classroom door. "Don't go without this!" She waved the poster in the air.

I grabbed it. Then we scrambled down the stairs and raced to the cafeteria. Just as we reached the entrance, Lauren skidded to a stop and seized my arm. "What's that noise?"

We both listened.

My stomach churned. "Screaming."

We raced inside. I was certain the mantis had attacked someone.

An apple whizzed by my head.

"Food fight!" someone shrieked.

Food fight? They were screaming about a food fight?

My eyes darted around the cafeteria, searching for the creature. "I see it," I whispered to Lauren. "It's wandering from table to table. And it's drooling like crazy."

"Who took my Twinkie?" a skinny, freckle-faced kid shouted.

"Who stole my peanut-butter-and-banana sandwich?" another kid yelled.

I watched the mantis grab a tub of cottage cheese and scoop up a big glob with its pincer. No one even noticed the tub hovering in the air. There was too much food flying around.

The mantis shoved a ball of the cottage cheese in its mouth—and spit it right back out. It flicked a chunk of it right into the lunchroom teacher's gray hair. Then it began to whip its pincer back and forth with fury, spattering white dots of cottage cheese everywhere.

"Yuck! Who's throwing this stuff?" a kid in a Dodgers baseball cap complained. "It's disgusting." He scraped it off his blue shirt and slung it at someone else.

"Is the mantis doing all this?" Lauren asked.

"Most of it," I answered. "I can't see too well. Corny still has my glasses." I can't wait till I get my hands on her, I muttered to myself.

"What is it doing right now?" she asked.

"It's weird, Lauren," I said as I squinted at it. "Its snatching food and sniffing it—and flinging it away. It isn't eating anything."

"Maybe it's not hungry," Lauren replied.

I shook my head. "It's hungry all right. It's dripping pools of drool. I just don't get it."

Suddenly I remembered the *Fun with Insects* book. I yanked it out of my back pocket. I flipped to the praying mantis page.

"Uh-oh," I moaned.

Lauren tried to read over my shoulder. "What, Wes? What?"

I took a deep breath. "According to this book, the mantis prefers its food alive."

"Alive?" Lauren's huge blue eyes grew wide. "As in walking, breathing alive?"

"Uh-huh."

PLOP. A big glob of carrots landed on my sneaker. Well, at least it doesn't have a cow eye in it, I thought as we both stared down at it—the

87

way the carrots did yesterday. I wished that day had never happened. Because that was the day I first saw the twins' Mystery Stereogram.

Why couldn't I see the mantis that day? I wondered. How come I could see it now? What was different? What—

"What's it doing now? What's it doing now?" Lauren interrupted my thoughts.

I searched the room. It was way in the back of the cafeteria. At that distance I couldn't see it at all.

CRASH!

A huge crash from the back. Followed by a long, terrifying scream.

"What's happening, Lauren? I can't see!"

"A table flipped over by itself!" Lauren yelled.

"I doubt it." We raced to the back of the cafeteria.

I really wish I had my glasses, I thought. "My glasses! That's it!" I shouted.

"What's going on?" Lauren asked the kids gathered around the upside-down table.

"Cornelia is trapped under there," a girl in a bright purple T-shirt answered.

"Yeah," Chad Miller added. "I tried to pull it off

her—but something cut me." He held up his hand. A deep jagged scratch ran across the back. "I couldn't see what it was. It was like—invisible or something." Chad shook his head, confused.

Lauren and I pushed through the crowd of kids—and there was Corny. Her legs were pinned under part of the table. But that wasn't what was holding her down. The mantis was draped across her chest!

Her hands thrashed the air as she screamed, "Get it off me!"

"Lauren! It's sitting on Corny. I have to get my glasses from her!"

"I know she's a total jerk. But shouldn't we help her before we worry about the glasses?" Lauren protested.

"No! I mean yes . . . I mean . . . the first time I saw the poster, I had my glasses on and everything was okay," I quickly explained. "But when I look at it without my glasses . . . I make it come alive. I think."

I stared down at Corny to check the mantis. A long strand of drool stretched from its mouth to the floor. And it was rubbing its front legs together—praying.

I shoved some kids aside and knelt next to Corny. The mantis started to rock back and forth.

"Give me my glasses," I ordered.

"First get me out of here," Corny screeched. "Something's on top of me! But I can't see it!"

I stared at her hard. "If you want to get out of here alive, give me my glasses. Now!"

Corny's face grew pale. The mantis was rocking. Rocking back and forth. Corny's eyes darted frantically to see what was pressing against her.

The mantis raised its pincers.

It opened its huge, gaping jaw.

A thick wad of drool oozed out on Corny's arm. Corny screamed.

"Now!" I yelled at her. "Now!"

"Here!" She slid my glasses out of her pocket.

I leaped up and shoved them on. I had only seconds before the mantis would strike.

I concentrated on the mantis.

Nothing happened.

"Is it working, Wes?" Lauren whispered.

"Ssh," I said. "I have to concentrate." Beads of sweat dripped down my face as I focused.

The mantis moved slightly. It was crouching.

Getting ready to spring.

To lunge for Corny's neck.

I stared as hard as I could.

My head ached.

My eyes throbbed and burned.

I wanted to close them. I needed to close them.

My eyelids started to drop—and then it happened.

Tiny dots began to appear. Hundreds of them. Thousands of them. Orange, green, pink, and yellow. Fluorescent dots all over the mantis's body.

They began to glow. Brighter and brighter.

Don't blink. Don't blink, I chanted to myself.

The dots began to swarm. They swirled and raced up and down the mantis's legs. All the way up its body. Up to its feelers. Up to its head.

Then the dots whirled apart. It was like watching an explosion in slow motion.

The dots flooded the cafeteria. Bouncing off the tables. The chairs. The kids. Buzzing. Buzzing.

And then they were gone.

Corny wiggled out from under the table. "Thanks for nothing, Wes," she muttered.

"Did it work?" Lauren asked softly.

I unrolled the poster clutched in my hand.

The blank space was—gone.

I breathed out the longest sigh of my life.

"It's back in the poster, Lauren."

"Yes! You were right!" she cried. "We're safe!"

"Not yet," I corrected her. "We're not safe until we destroy this poster for good."

15

"The scissors are in the top drawer, next to the refrigerator," I told Lauren. We had a long talk when we got home from school about the best way to get rid of the mantis. This was all we could think of.

"Are you sure it's safe?" Lauren asked.

"I hope so," I said.

I read a note stuck to the refrigerator. "Mom says she and Dad took Vicky shopping. So this is the best time."

I made certain my glasses were firmly in place. Then I rolled the poster out on the kitchen table.

Lauren handed me the scissors.

I laughed nervously. "My hands are shaking."

I swallowed hard. "Here goes." I turned the poster from side to side, trying to decide where to cut. Actually I was stalling. I didn't know what would happen if I cut the poster. Would the mantis burst out if I sliced through the dots?

I squeezed my eyes shut and snipped into the paper. I did it really quickly. I was scared.

No buzzing.

I opened my eyes and snipped again. This time I cut the poster in half.

"Think it worked?" Lauren asked.

I stared down at the two pieces. "I don't know."

"Are you going to make sure?" she asked.

I nodded. "I guess I have to."

"Be careful. Have your glasses ready," Lauren warned.

My stomach clenched. "I will." I slid my glasses down my nose. Then I peeked over the top of them at the left half of the poster.

I jerked my head away and shoved my glasses up. "It's still there," I groaned.

"Okay, okay," Lauren said. "Let's stay calm." But she didn't sound calm. "Maybe we just need to cut it in smaller pieces."

94

Lauren picked up the scissors. "I'll do it this time." She made a tiny cut, then glanced over at me. "Turn around, okay? It makes me nervous when you stare at the poster—even with your glasses on."

I turned away from the kitchen table.

Snip. Snip. Snip. I grew more and more nervous with each little snip.

I heard Lauren slam the scissors down on the table. Then I heard a tearing sound.

"What are you doing?" I asked.

"I'm ripping it up. It's quicker than the scissors," she explained.

Riiiip. I hated that sound even more than the scissor snips. A drop of sweat rolled down my cheek. I wiped my clammy hands on my jeans.

I heard Lauren rip the paper again and again and again.

What if it's still there?

What if we're only making things worse?

What if we're making the mantis *angry?*

"That ought to do it," she announced. "You can turn around now."

I whirled to face her—and gasped. A mound of paper filled the center of the table. Tiny pieces about the size of the fingernail on my pinky.

95

Lauren's face flushed pink. "I didn't want to take any chances."

"I guess I should check it again," I said. I hoped she would say I didn't have to.

But she nodded. I knew she was right. We had to be sure the creature was really gone.

I pulled my glasses down to the end of my nose. The pieces were so tiny. I could barely see them.

I leaned over the table.

I still couldn't be sure.

A drop of sweat ran down my chin and plopped onto the pile.

I bent my head lower and lower. Closer and closer.

The blood pounded in my ears.

"Be careful not to—"

Before Lauren could finish her warning, it was too late.

A tiny pincer lashed out at my face.

My glasses went flying.

I heard them hit the floor.

"Lauren! Get my glasses!" I yelled.

"Where did they go?" she cried, searching the floor on her hands and knees.

"I don't know!" I answered. "Hurry!"

Tiny legs burst out of each piece of the poster.

Tiny eyes glared up at me.

Sharp little pincers clicked open and shut.

They swarmed over the table.

Hundreds.

Hundreds of miniature praying mantises!

16

"They're back!"

"Huh? They?" Lauren shrieked.

"They're pouring out of all the pieces!" I cried.

"Oh, no!" Lauren moaned. "What do we do now?"

"We've got to find my glasses!"

"I'm checking under the table," she called.

"Wait!" I yelled. But it was too late.

The mantises marched down the table legs— toward Lauren. The kitchen filled with their horrible buzzing.

I grabbed a dish towel from the counter and whipped it at the little monsters.

"Get out of there! The mantises are headed right for you!"

Lauren scrambled out from under the table. "They're on me! They're on me!" she cried, jumping up and down. "I think they're in my hair!" She leaned forward and slapped at her head.

"Hold still!" I yelled at her. "Let me look!" The buzzing grew louder and louder. I could hardly think.

She shook her head violently. "I can't hold still, Wes. I just can't! Do something! Please!"

I grabbed her head to hold it still. The green insects swarmed over her hair—burrowing deeper and deeper.

I tried to pick them out, but it was impossible. They lashed out with their sharp pincers. "Quick! Go to the sink!"

"Water!" Lauren shouted. "Perfect. We'll drown them."

Then I turned on the cold tap full force and guided Lauren's head under it.

I turned to check the table. "Oh, no!" I spotted a mantis launch off the table and soar into the air. "They can fly."

"It's not working," Lauren called from the sink. "I can feel them. They're starting to bite!"

"No, it is working, Lauren," I said, peering at her head. "I can see them spilling off."

I felt a sharp sting on the back of my neck. Then on my forehead. My nose. One of my ears.

The mantises swarmed around my head.

Dodged at my face.

Clawed into my skin.

I stumbled backward, pawing frantically at my head.

Then I heard a terrifying sound.

And I knew we were doomed.

17

CRUNCH.

I heard a crunch. Underfoot.

And I knew what I had stepped on. With a sinking feeling I snatched my glasses up from the floor. Maybe only one lens broke, I silently wished. Maybe only one.

Nope.

Both of them—smashed.

Yes. We're both doomed, I thought.

I grabbed the dish towel again. This time I threw it over my head, trying to protect myself from the stinging creatures.

Think, Wes. Think, I ordered myself. They are bugs. How do you get rid of bugs?

I dashed to the wall switch and flicked on the ceiling light.

Yes! The mantises flew toward the light and began to circle. A few bounced off the bulb and dropped to the table. Then they staggered up and launched themselves at the glowing bulb again.

They were under control. For now.

Lauren pulled her head out from under the tap. Water streamed down her long hair. Down her face. "Where are they?"

I pointed to the ceiling light.

Lauren grinned. "Great! Now all we have to do is find your glasses!"

"Uh. I already did," I admitted. I held them up.

"Oh, no! Now what do we do?" Lauren wailed. "Do you have an extra pair?"

"That *was* my extra pair," I answered.

I peered up at the insects, squinting into the light. The buzzing noise suddenly changed to a low humming sound.

My eyes felt itchy, but I kept staring—because I noticed a small change.

"Something's happening," I murmured.

"What?" Lauren grabbed my arm. "What's happening. Tell me!"

"They're changing."

"Changing? How?" Lauren demanded. "They're not growing, are they? Please, don't tell me they're growing."

"No. They're definitely not growing. But they're not getting smaller, either." I blinked several times. "They're turning into those dots. It's just like what happened in the cafeteria!"

"Yes!" Lauren cried. "That means they're disappearing!"

"I don't think so, Lauren."

"Well, what are they doing?" she cried.

"They're still up there. Humming. Orange, pink, yellow, and green humming dots," I explained. "Now they're swirling around the light. Really fast. The colors are almost melting together."

"Maybe they're dying," Lauren suggested.

"No!" I exclaimed. "No! They're forming one big ball of color now! One big ball of green!"

"Oh, n-noooo," Lauren wailed. "Look!"

I ripped my eyes away from the swirling green ball of color.

"Look!" Lauren cried again, pointing to the table with a trembling hand. "The poster," she croaked.

I shifted my gaze to the table.

The pile of tiny paper scraps had vanished.

The poster had grown back—in one whole piece.

With the big white mantis-shaped spot in the middle.

18

I raised my eyes to the green ball.

It fell to the floor with a dull thump.

Two black feelers thrust out of the top.

Six long bristly legs burst out of the back.

The pincers on the front legs snapped open and closed.

"Get out!" I yelled at Lauren. "Get out while you can! The mantis is back!"

"I'm staying!" she shouted. "Where is it? What should I do?"

"It's coming this way. Circle around the table

and stand on the other side of the room. Maybe it won't be able to decide which of us to go for!"

Lauren slid around the table. "What's it doing now? Do you think it's going to attack?"

I backed up until I hit the wall. "It's so close I can't move." I gulped. "It's in a praying position."

"Wes, play dead!" Lauren cried. "It wants to eat food that's still alive!"

I slumped onto the floor and rolled my eyes back in my head. I tried to hold my breath.

For a second nothing happened. Then I felt the mantis's cold feelers probing my neck.

It's trying to decide if I'm alive, I thought. If I move a muscle, it will attack.

I could feel its hot breath on my cheek.

Its saliva drip down my face.

My eyelids twitched as its creepy pincers crawled along my skin.

I wanted to bat it away.

Don't move. Don't move.

I wanted to breathe. My chest felt tight. My lungs were about to burst.

Don't move! Don't move!

Slowly I felt the mantis slide away. I heard him slither in his drool across the kitchen floor.

I opened one eye.

I couldn't spot the mantis. Where was it?

My lungs were definitely going to explode now. I took a tiny breath. Then I opened my other eye and lifted my head slightly off the floor.

Now I could see it.

But Lauren couldn't. She was watching me. Biting her lip. Twisting her hands together. Worrying about me.

And there was the mantis—standing next to her. Standing next to Lauren—who was breathing. Moving. Alive.

I slowly pushed myself off the floor.

"Don't move!" I mouthed.

Lauren understood.

I crept over to the mantis. Slowly. Very slowly.

It was perched next to the stove. Rocking back and forth.

Rubbing its pincers together.

"Hey, what are you guys doing? Why are you crawling on the floor?" a voice called from the doorway.

Vicky.

The mantis snapped its head toward my sister. I grabbed Lauren's arm and pulled her away from the huge insect.

"Wow! Your glasses are ruined," Vicky said,

lifting the broken frames from the table. "Wes, you're in major trouble!"

The mantis's feelers waved with fury. Its eyes darted from me to Lauren to Vicky and back.

"I've never broken my glasses," Vicky bragged. "Never even lost them. Wait until Mom and Dad see." She pushed her glasses up.

I slid along the wall toward her. Then I jumped up, grabbed her glasses off her face, and pushed her away.

"Hey, what are you doing?" she yelled. "Those are mine!"

She tried to snatch them back.

"Ssh!" I warned. I held them high over my head.

She hopped up and down, but she couldn't reach them.

"Vicky, wait outside. I'll give them back in a minute," I promised.

"I'm not leaving without my glasses!" Vicky folded her arms in front of her. "And you'd better not break them!"

I forced her glasses on my face. They were way too small. They pinched my nose. And they didn't quite reach my ears.

"You look stupid," Vicky said.

"Quiet!" I warned. I had to concentrate.

I stared at the mantis.

I moved closer to it and stared really hard.

I strained to see every detail.

Focus. Focus. Don't blink.

I moved in closer.

I stared.

Disappear. Please—disappear back into the poster.

This *has* to work, I told myself. It *has* to.

But the mantis didn't move.

19

"**T**he glasses aren't working!" I moaned. "They're just not working."

The mantis lashed out—so fast I didn't see it coming. But I felt it.

It had me by the neck. Choking off my air.

Its pincers raked my skin.

Its huge eyes gleamed greedily into mine.

Its jaws snapped open and shut. Then it lifted me right off the floor.

Lauren and Vicky gasped as I rose up.

"He's floating!" Vicky cried.

I kicked helplessly.

"Wes, you're scaring me!" Vicky cried.

"Keep staring, Wes! Keep staring!" Lauren yelled.

I gazed directly into the mantis's face. Colors swirled through its deep black eyes. Its eyes looked like two giant kaleidoscopes now. Swirling colors in orange, pink, yellow, green.

Swirling colors!

Colored dots!

"It's working!" I cried. "I think it's working!"

Vicky's glasses *were* working. They were weaker than mine—so they were just taking longer!

Fluorescent dots began to race over the mantis's legs and feelers. Over its whole body!

Then the dots drifted apart.

I crumpled to the floor, but I kept Vicky's glasses pressed against my face.

Dots bounced off the refrigerator. They hit the screen door. They whirled and swirled like mini-tornadoes through the kitchen.

"Give me my glasses back now," Vicky whined. "You're acting crazy."

"Just one more minute, Vicky," I begged. "One more minute." I knew I had almost defeated it.

"Wes! The poster!" Lauren exclaimed, dashing over to the table.

I forced myself up and peered over her shoulder.

The white mantis-shaped spot had filled in with color. The mantis was back where he belonged.

Sal had definitely been right. Some things *are* better left in two dimensions.

I collapsed into a kitchen chair.

"We won! We won!" Lauren cheered.

"Not yet." I sighed. "We still have to get rid of the poster."

"Give me my glasses back, Wes." Vicky stomped her feet on the floor.

"Not yet, Vicky," I murmured.

"I'll get Mom and Dad. They'll make you."

"Where are Mom and Dad?" I asked.

"They're outside in the front yard burning a pile of leaves," Vicky replied. Then she ran out, slamming the screen door behind her.

I turned to Lauren and smiled. I eyed the poster. "Let's burn it!"

"Yesss!" Lauren held up her palm and we high-fived.

We dashed out to the front yard. "Hi, Mom!" I called. "Where's Dad?"

"He's in the back, collecting more leaves," she answered. "Wes, what are you doing with your sister's glasses?" Vicky stood beside her—squinting at me triumphantly.

"Uhhh. It's part of a science project," I blurted out.

"For Mr. Gosling's class. Optics," Lauren added.

"Please let me wear them for five more minutes, Vicky," I pleaded.

"Let your brother wear them for a few minutes, Vicky. It's for school."

Vicky dug her foot into the dirt and kicked a chunk of it on my jeans.

"Come on, Vicky," Mom said, wrapping an arm around her shoulder. "Let's help Dad with the leaves in the backyard. Then we'll all go in and have some ice cream."

"Can I throw them into the fire? Can I have chocolate-banana-chunk? Can I give Clawd some?"

"No, yes, and yes," Mom replied as they made their way around back.

I peered up at the sky. It was almost dark. A full orange moon glowed above.

I turned to Lauren. "Okay," I said. "Here goes nothing." I tossed the poster into the center of the fire.

The flames caught on the edge of the poster. Then there was a bang—like a firecracker shooting off.

Lauren and I jumped back.

"Guess we're kind of nervous." Lauren giggled nervously. "I don't see anything weird happening. Do you?"

"No," I answered. Then I sniffed the air. It suddenly smelled bad. Really bad. Like the mantis's sour breath.

The fire engulfed the poster now. Furious flames shot through it and licked the sky.

Smoke began to stream from the center of the leaf pile. Greenish-gray smoke. It rose fast—in a long, straight ribbon.

Then I heard the high-pitched buzzing. Louder. Louder. Louder. I wanted to cover my ears. But I had to hold Vicky's glasses on.

Lauren glanced at me. "You okay?" she asked. I nodded.

The smoke drifted higher in the sky. Drifted past the full, bright, orange moon. Then it began to curl.

The smoke curled and curled—into the form of a perfect praying mantis. Huge and dark, it floated in front of the moon.

Then it disappeared.

I turned to Lauren. "Did you see that?" I asked.

"See what?" she said.

"Never mind," I replied.

No one else could see the mantis.

No one else could hear its terrible buzzing.

No one else could make it come alive.

The mantis was my own private nightmare.

A nightmare in 3-D.

And it was over.

Or was it?

20

Two weeks later Lauren came home from school with me. We planned to do some homework together.

"Wes, you got a package today," Mom said when she walked into the kitchen. She set down a cylinder-shaped package on the kitchen table.

Lauren and I exchanged glances.

"The Mystery Prize!" we cried together.

We both dropped our pencils.

I picked the package up. I checked out the return address. "It's from the poster company," I told Lauren. "It's definitely my prize."

"Open it!" Lauren said.

I tore the wrapping off one end and slid the prize out of the cylinder.

"I can't believe it! Another poster!" I said. I rolled it open on the table.

"Oh, no!" Lauren gasped. "Careful, Wes," she said under her breath.

"Another stereogram?" Mom asked, looking over our shoulders. "Is that the prize? Can you see it, Lauren?"

Lauren squinted at the poster. "Uh-uh. I can't see a thing," she said. "Just those black and brown lines."

Mom spent a long time staring at it. But she couldn't make it out, either.

"Hey, what's up? Cool! Whose poster? What is it? Can I have a look?" It was Vicky, of course.

"Sure, have a look," I said, shoving the poster toward her.

"Nope. Can't see a thing. Mom, what's for dinner? Can I have a snack now? Please? Where's Clawd?"

"Pizza. No. In the backyard," Mom told Vicky.

Lauren moved closer. "Are you going to try to see it?" she whispered.

"Do you think I should?" I asked.

Lauren shrugged. "Might as well. We know how to control it, don't we?"

I leaned on the table and looked over the top of my glasses.

It took me only a few seconds to see it.

It was big.

And hairy.

And coming straight at me.

A gigantic tarantula scurried out from under a rock and reached a hairy leg right out of the poster.

I jumped backward and nearly fell over Vicky.

"Wes!" Mom cried. "What on earth is wrong with you?"

"Nothing, Mom. It's okay," I replied. I rolled the poster up as fast as I could. "Lauren, can you give me a hand with these books?" I asked.

When we got upstairs, I told her. "There's a monster in the poster. A huge tarantula. And, Lauren," I whispered, "it wants to get out!"

"Come on, Fluffy!" came a voice from next door.

Lauren and I peered out the window.

I saw Gabby. She and Corny were playing with Fluffums. This was the game: They had a stuffed cat, white like Clawd. It had a collar around its neck and a leash. They were dragging the stuffed cat in a circle. They were urging Fluffums to chase it and catch it.

"Come on, Fluff," Corny instructed. "Get that nasty old cat."

Fluffums went running after the cat. He grabbed it and chewed on its neck, growling.

"Good boy!" Gabby cried, patting the dog.

It made me feel sick.

"I'm really starting to dislike that family," Lauren said.

The twins stared up at us. "Hey, where is your cross-eyed cat?" Corny called.

"Yeah, Fluffums wants to play!" Gabby added.

They were both twirling their ponytails and smirking.

I turned to Lauren. "I bet I can make them promise to keep that little hairball away from Clawd from now on."

I leaned out the window. "Hey, you guys, I forgot to tell you!" I shouted. "I won the prize. I solved the Mystery Stereogram."

"Yeah, for sure!" Gabby said, rolling her eyes.

"No way," Corny added.

I sighed and ducked back in the window.

"Bet they'd just love to see my prize," I said. I

tapped the tarantula poster on my hand. "Maybe I'll even give it to them."

"Good idea," Lauren replied, grinning evilly. "I'll hold your glasses this time. You don't want to break another pair."

"Corny! Gabby!" I called out the window. "Wait right there. I have a really cool surprise for you!"

ARE YOU READY FOR ANOTHER WALK
DOWN FEAR STREET?
TURN THE PAGE FOR A TERRIFYING
SNEAK PREVIEW.

R.L. STINE'S

GHOSTS OF
FEAR STREET ®

STAY AWAY FROM
THE TREE HOUSE

I was shivering.

But that was a good sign!

Yes. Cold was definitely a good sign.

Because cold spots meant ghosts!

"Do you see anything?" my brother Steve whispered in my ear.

"No—wait. Maybe." I stared hard at the big oak tree. "There!" I pointed. "I just saw a light on that side of the tree. Then it went out."

I dug my heels into the ground—planting them there firmly—so it would be harder to bolt, which is exactly what I wanted to do.

I cleared my throat.

"Who is there?" My voice squeaked.

The light flashed again.

Then it went out.

Crunch, crunch, crunch.

"D-did you hear that?" I asked Steve. He nodded.

Something was moving in the dark.

Crunch, crunch, crunch.

There it was again. Moving. Toward us.

I swung the flashlight around wildly. Trying to catch it in my beam.

Then I heard another sound. A voice. A laugh.

"Steve, did you hear that?" I whispered. "It laughed."

"Shine your light over there," Steve whispered back.

He sounded scared. I knew I was.

I swung my flashlight in its direction—and two human-like forms walked toward us.

Girls.

Two girls squinting in the light and giggling.

Two totally alive girls.

I wanted a ghost. Or a werewolf. Or a vampire. Even a mummy.

But no. I found girls.

"Who are you?" Steve asked as we walked toward them. "What are you doing out here?"

"I'm Kate Drennan," one of the girls answered in a soft voice. "And this is my sister, Betsy."

Both girls had bright blue eyes and long black hair. The one named Kate had straight hair tied back in a ponytail. The other one had wavy hair with curls that tumbled all the way down her back.

I'd never seen either of them before—even though they looked as though they should be in my grade.

"We were just—" Kate began again. But before she could finish, Betsy cut her off.

"Why do you get to ask the questions?" she demanded. "We have as much right to be here as you do."

"Okay, okay," I started to apologize. "It's just that I've never seen you around here before. Do you go to Shadyside Middle School?"

"No," Kate started to answer.

"We're on spring break," Betsy interrupted. "We go to school in Vermont. We don't know many kids in Shadyside, so it gets pretty boring."

"That's why we sneaked out tonight," Kate added. "We were bored. There was nothing on TV. Nothing to do."

"We sneaked out, too," I admitted.

Kate—the quieter one—smiled. And Betsy—the bossy one—seemed to relax a little.

"At least you get a vacation," Steve added. "We don't have one until school lets out for the summer."

"We should head back," Betsy said. "Our parents might check up on us or something."

"Us, too. We'll probably see you around," I volunteered. "We'll be out here a lot—we're going to rebuild that tree house."

I shone the flashlight up into the branches of the big dark oak. Both girls glanced up. Then I noticed Kate's expression. She looked scared. Really scared.

Betsy glared at me. "What did you say?" she asked.

"I said we're going to rebuild that old tree house."

"That's what I thought you said," Betsy replied. "But you can't."

"Why can't we?" Steve demanded.

"No one can," Betsy insisted.

Kate began chewing nervously on the end of her ponytail. "You can't rebuild the tree house," she said. "You can't because . . . because . . ."

"Because of the secret about it," Betsy finished for her sister.

"The secret?" I asked. "What secret?"

A tree house with a secret! Is this cool or what?

"We can't tell you. Everyone knows about this old tree house," Betsy snapped.

Then she narrowed her eyes. "But I *will* tell you this—if you don't want to get hurt . . . you'll stay away from the tree house!"

"They're just trying to scare us," Steve replied. "But it's not going to work. Right?"

"Right," I replied, not feeling as convinced as I sounded.

"Well, I—uh—really think you should listen to Betsy," Kate whispered. "Because we, um, we heard some kids tried to fix up the tree house and they . . ."

"What happened to them?" These girls were driving me crazy. "Did they die? What happened?"

Betsy shook her sister's shoulder, interrupting her for the millionth time. "Come on. Let's go. They don't need to hear that old story," she snapped. "If they're smart, they'll just stay away."

"Why? Why should we stay away?" I asked.

Then I remembered what I read about ghosts and cold spots. "Wow! I said. "Is the tree house haunted?"

"Come on, Kate," Betsy ordered. "These guys are hopeless."

Kate gave sort of a half smile. "We do have to go," she said. "Our mom will freak if she can't find us."

"Wait!" I protested. "Just tell us some more about the tree house. Please!"

I thought Kate was about to say something, but Betsy didn't give her a chance. "I said come *on,*" she grumbled, tugging her sister across the clearing.

"Bye," Kate called over her shoulder.

As they stepped onto the path, Betsy stopped and called back, "Remember, you have been warned. Now if anything bad happens to you, it will be your own fault!"

The next day at school, I couldn't concentrate. Betsy's warning kept echoing in my head. What did it mean? What was the big secret about the tree house?

It must be haunted, I decided. That had to be it. At least I hoped so.

I spent the last part of the day—the part when we were supposed to be doing math—drawing tree house plans on the cover of my notebook.

In some of the plans, I sketched a shadowy figure sitting on the end of a branch. I made it shadowy because I didn't know what a ghost really looked like. Not yet, anyway.

As soon as the last bell rang, I raced home. I headed straight into the garage and loaded up two big cardboard boxes with nails, old boards, and lots of tools.

That was the easy part.

Next came the hard part—Steve. I found him lying on the couch, watching TV and munching Cheese Curlies.

"Come on," I said. "We have to start before it gets too dark out there."

Steve's eyes remained glued to the screen. "Let's wait till Saturday," he answered. "I want to watch the rest of this show."

I glanced at the TV. "You've seen that cartoon at least one hundred times!" I snatched the remote from his hand and clicked off the TV. "We had a deal."

"Our deal didn't say *when* I had to help," Steve answered. "What's the big rush, anyway?"

"I think the tree house is haunted! I think someone died up there! And I did see something in the shadows."

"Dylan," Steve said, shaking his head, "the only thing that died is your brain."

"I can *prove* to you that ghosts are real," I replied. "Just think about it—this is the perfect chance for us to settle our argument about ghosts. If the tree house is haunted, I know I can prove it."

Steve shoved himself up from the sofa.

"All right, Dylan, my lad. But if we don't see a ghost before we finish the tree house, you have to admit I was right and you were wrong."

"Sure. Let's go."

"And you have to stop talking about ghosts, reading about ghosts, watching movies about ghosts—even thinking about ghosts. Deal?" Steve asked.

"Deal," I agreed.

We headed to the garage to pick up the supplies. Steve chose the lightest box, of course.

We cut across the backyard, and I led the way into the woods. "Wow!" Steve cried as he stumbled along behind me. "The woods are even colder than last night. From now on, I'm wearing my winter parka when we come out here."

"It's because of the ghost," I informed him. "Haunted places usually have a colder temperature."

"Give me a break!" Steve shouted. "It's cold because of all the trees. The sunlight can't get through the branches."

After that we trudged along without talking. My box felt heavier with every step. I thought about turning around and asking Steve to trade. But I didn't want to start another argument.

I stopped when the path reached the clearing.

I scanned the shadows around the oak tree.

Nothing there.

I dumped my cardboard box on the ground. I turned to Steve—and couldn't believe what I saw. "Where's yours?" I demanded.

"Where's my what?" Steve asked, smiling.

"Your *box*."

Steve took off his baseball cap, smoothed his hair, and stuck the cap back on. "I left it at the edge of the backyard. We couldn't possibly use all that junk in one day," Steve explained.

"That was not our deal!" I yelled. "Our deal was that you help. Watching me carry a box does not count as help. And neither does leaving our stuff behind!"

"Okay, okay. I'll get the box," Steve muttered.

I watched Steve disappear down the path—and realized what a big mistake I had made. I'd be lucky if Steve returned—with or without the box.

In fact, I knew exactly what Steve would do. He would decide he needed a glass of water. No, a glass of water and some more Cheese Curlies—to build up his strength. And since he couldn't eat and carry the box at the same time, he'd watch a few cartoons until he finished the Curlies. And by then, it would be time for me to go home.

Well, I didn't need Steve, anyway. I really didn't expect him to do much work. I just wanted him along because the woods were kind of creepy. Which is exactly what I started thinking as I opened the carton.

It was quiet here. Way too quiet.

And dark. Steve was right about the branches. They blocked out all the sunlight.

I glanced up at the tree house and felt a shiver race up and down my spine. You wanted to see a ghost, I told myself. And now's your chance.

I forced myself to march over to the tree. I tested the first rung of the ladder nailed onto the trunk. A little wobbly, but okay, I decided.

I stepped on the rung. It held me—no problem. I tugged on the second rung before I climbed up— it felt okay, too. Only three more rungs to go.

I stared up at the tree house again. An icy breeze swept over me and my knees began to shake.

Take a deep breath, I told myself. Don't wimp out now.

I stepped up to the next rung.

And that's when I heard the sound.

A sickening CRACK.

My feet flew out from under me as the third rung snapped off the trunk.

I flung my arms around the trunk. I kicked my legs wildly, searching for the next rung.

My heart pounded in my chest until my feet found it. Then I clung there for a few minutes. Hugging the tree trunk tightly, trying to catch my breath.

A cold gust of wind blew. My teeth began to chatter.

I inhaled deeply. "Okay, just one more rung to go," I said out loud. But I couldn't move. I remained frozen to the spot.

Then I pictured myself talking to Steve after I'd proven that ghosts exist. "Steve, my lad," I would say, "don't feel stupid. Even though you are a year older, no one expects you to be right about everything."

That gave me the courage to go on.

I made my way to the top rung. I peered underneath the tree house and studied the platform. Half of it was badly damaged. The boards were black and charred. But the other half appeared solid enough. I banged on it with my fist a few times just to make sure.

Then I pulled myself through the open trapdoor—and felt something touch my face. Something soft. Something airy. Something light.

I screamed.

I found the ghost!